Home to Mackinac

Home to Mackinac

The Tale of Young Jack Murphy's Discovery of Loyalty, Family and Forgiveness

by Kim Delmar Cory

illustrated by Laura Evans

Mackinac Island, Michigan

Home to Mackinac

The Tale of Young Jack Murphy's Discovery of Loyalty, Family and Forgiveness

Written by Kim Delmar Cory

Illustrated by Laura Evans

Mackinac State Historic Parks
Mackinac Island, Michigan 49757

Printed in the United States of America

First printing 4,000 copies

Library of Congress Cataloging-in-Publication Data

Cory, Kim Delmar.
Home to Mackinac : the tale of young Jack Murphy's discovery of loyalty, family and forgiveness / by Kim Delmar Cory ; illustrated by Laura Evans.—1st ed.
p. cm.
Summary: In 1885, fourteen-year-old Jack, homeless after the sale of the Ohio farm belonging to his recently deceased paternal grandparents, travels with his dog to Michigan's Mackinac Island to search for the sister he barely knows and to resolve the mystery surrounding the long-ago disappearance of their father, a soldier at the nearby fort.
ISBN-13: 978-0-911872-87-3 (pbk.)
ISBN-10: 0-911872-87-6 (pbk.)
[1. Identity—Fiction. 2. Family—Fiction. 3. Brothers and sisters—Fiction. 4. Metis—Fiction. 5. Mackinac Island (Mich.)—History—19th century—Fiction.] I. Evans, Laura, 1963- ill. II. Title.
PZ7.C8174Ho 2006
[Fic]—dc22

2006001491

Dedication

I dedicate this book to my husband, Loren, and my children, Amanda and Justin, who share my enchantment with the magic of Mackinac Island.

And to my Nana, who is with me always.

Publication of this book was made
possible by a generous gift from

Mackinac Associates
Friends Preserving Mackinac's Heritage

Prologue

Spring 1885

I hope I find her, thought Jack.

He pulled his jacket closer against the brisk April wind. Jack Murphy liked knowing what to expect.

He liked farming because he knew if seeds were planted in the spring, tended to by him and his grandpa through the summer, a crop would be harvested come fall.

He liked his hotcakes and sausage with toast smothered in orange marmalade that his grandma fixed him every morning. He even liked milking the cows, Kate and Beulah, before breakfast.

Jack liked waking to a rooster crowing every morning.

He liked knowing sun dried clean sheets would cover his bed every other Saturday. And come fall, a dance would be held to celebrate harvest time. Where he could watch pretty blonde Constance Morrow sashay and flirt across the floor in floppy pink ribbons and bows while he played his fiddle from the safety of the barn loft.

Yet here he stood. On the steam boat *Algomah*, the island called Mackinac within view. Smelling lake air for the first time.

Alone for the first time in his fourteen years. Except for the golden mass of fur thumping his tail on the deck.

Pocketing his hands for warmth, Jack touched his train ticket stub. The ticket that originally had Boston printed on the destination. Until Jack had found himself standing at the train station ticket window having it stamped for Detroit instead.

Jack knew he wasn't where he was supposed to be now.

But he was where he had to be.

Could it have been only a week ago that Jack had sat by his grandmother's deathbed in Ohio as she mumbled her last prayers?

That he'd watched her practiced fingers run through her prayers with the pale green smoothness of her rosary?

Heard her quiet confessions echoing within his ears?

— I —

"Truth and lies"

The stone walls of Fort Mackinac high above the village glimmered in the soft April sunshine, white like the seagulls soaring and squawking overhead. Sailboats and rowboats bobbed in the harbor. A whisper of snow floated in front of Jack's face.

Fool barked and Jack ruffled his golden fur.

As the ferry approached the island, Fool trotted back and forth.

Jack felt restless too. He pictured the last photo he'd seen of his father, red haired and smiling in his blue soldier uniform. It had been taken before Jack was born.

Through fluttering snowflakes, Jack noticed that several overturned rowboats dotted the narrow beach. Mackinac Village to his left seemed larger as the steamship approached the island, docking at a long wooden pier.

Workers yelled at the crew to secure the lines.

The houses on the street below and to the right of the massive fort looked bigger and fancier than the town buildings, thought Jack. He watched a black trotting horse pull a fine black surrey down a street.

Jack hoisted the large leather bag across his shoulder, adjusting the fiddle strapped to his back. He shrugged for comfort. All he had in life lay heavy across his shoulders. Except for Fool.

"Fool!" he yelled as the dog bounded down the wooden gangplank.

Fool circled to meet his master, his long fluffy tail thudding against the dock.

A sinking sun painted the island roofs a tender shade of yellow and Jack thought it a pretty place. Mostly wooden buildings, some brown, some white, some barn red, some large and some small lined the main street off the dock. Jack noted this street was called Water Street. He would need to learn his way around.

Three soldiers walked up the dirt street in the direction of the fort. A woman holding a tottering boy by the hand and a brown wrapped parcel under her arm passed in front of him.

Jack wondered if his mother had ever held his hand like that.

Commanding Fool to stay with him, Jack walked down the street. His heavy boots clumped on the wooden boardwalk. He read the signs on many storefronts: Indian Curiosities, Moose Hair, Sweet-Grass Work including canoes, satchels, and miniature mococks of Maple Sugar. Most boasted tour guides and the natural wonders of Mackinac Island. Patting a panting Fool, Jack wondered at this place.

Never had he seen anything like this in Ohio.

He shivered before stopping in front of a store that offered a large assortment of Drugs and Medicines. And Ice-Cold Soda-Water.

For some strange reason Jack was surprised that he recognized himself in the window reflection. He didn't feel the same as he had a week ago. So it figured he wouldn't look the same. But there he was– the same reddish brown curls spilling over his tan jacket collar, olive skin that never freckled even under the midsummer sun, sharp cheekbones and a strong straight nose. The same dark blue eyes his grandma had always called 'China blue'.

Jack could never figure out what China had to do with his eyes.

Loud and uneven bugle sounds from the fort drew his attention. He wondered if it was calling the soldiers to their supper. His rumbling stomach gurgled, making Fool's ears cock with interest.

Emptiness rushed through Jack, swallowing him like storm clouds swallow the sun. He felt like he was watching himself from a far place.

Maybe that's what his grandparents were doing right now, Jack thought. Watching him from heaven.

He checked his inside jacket pocket. Still there.

He watched a tiny snowflake melt into the store window

and for a second he felt a kinship with it.

The life he knew was gone. Home was gone. He would have to melt into a new life. Somehow. Somewhere.

The farm, house and Grandpa's farm equipment would all be sold. Pete, the gentle old plow horse, would live out the rest of his days in a neighbor's pasture. Jack had made that arrangement himself before leaving.

With a slight nod, Jack confirmed his choice for Pete. And for himself. Coming here was the right thing.

He sighed.

It had to be.

Tugging at his cap brim, he entered the store.

Woven mats and baskets filled with corn husk dolls lined the floor along the counter. Snow shoes and pipes hung from the center pole. Floor to ceiling wooden shelves cluttered with canned goods and every type of curing potion, hair balm, or tonic imaginable covered the walls. Brightly colored penny candy and licorice whips filled square glass jars lining the front counter. The smell of camphor penetrated Jack's nose as he entered, making him sneeze.

"God Bless you," came a voice from above.

A balding older man wearing a white shirt and apron, brown and white striped pants and a droopy sand colored mustache was climbing down a ladder leaning against a top shelf.

"Thank you," said Jack.

Starting to wipe his nose on his sleeve, Jack thought better of it. When he raised his head from his arm, he spotted Hall's Hair Tonic on the shelf behind the bald man. His throat tightened. Jack recalled following his grandpa into Parson's General Store when he was much younger in their small Ohio town of Kendall Plains. When they left, Grandpa had his hair tonic and Jack gripped penny candy in his little hand.

"Help you, young man?" the shopkeeper repeated, wiping his hands on his apron.

Jack realized the man had greeted him for the second time.

The shopkeeper gestured at the fiddle strapped across Jack's back. "You play?"

Jack shrugged and looked away. "Some."

Fool's face filled the door window. Jack pulled two nickels from his pocket.

"Could I buy a soda water and a root beer, sir?"

"Thirsty?" asked the shopkeeper, smiling as he retrieved and opened the beverages.

"The water's for my dog." Jack gestured at Fool's face in the window.

"There's water in the troughs out front," the shopkeeper indicated through the window.

"He doesn't like that water."

The man shook his head.

"Finicky dog." The shopkeeper didn't sound too happy but he smiled. "I suppose you'll be needing a bowl then. Be right back."

Jack looked around the store, stopping when he saw the Whitman Candy display.

He thought back to late last summer. It had been his grandmother's birthday. He and his grandpa had been picking up supplies in town and Jack wanted to buy her something special. He'd spent half his saved money on a large yellow box of Whitman chocolates. He smiled with memory. She'd cried and kept her trinkets in it when it was finally emptied, saying what a shame it would be to throw out such a fine box.

Jack figured the box and its contents had likely been thrown out when the neighbor ladies had cleaned his grandparent's closet a few days ago.

The shopkeeper returned. Holding the bottles by the necks with one hand, Jack took the offered bowl.

"You, uh, your folks around?" the man asked.

Jack shrugged. "No, Sir."

The man waited, expecting more. But Jack was not one to say more than was needed.

Placing the bowl under one arm, he walked to the door.

"Sir," he faced the shopkeeper before turning the knob. "Do you know where I might find a girl named Maggie? Maggie Murphy?"

Jack listened to the rhythm of her name. He'd never said it out loud before. Never knew she existed before last week.

"Murphy?" The shopkeeper was sweeping. "Think she might work over at Astor House. Young, long dark hair?"

Jack shrugged.

"Try Astor House over on Market Street." The shopkeeper stopped sweeping to point. "A street over."

Jack thanked the man and left. It no longer snowed. Dusk descended, purple and tangerine clouds gathering along the horizon like giant mounds of bread dough. Out on the boardwalk, he poured the water for Fool who lapped the bowl dry then flopped down. Jack shoved the bowl inside the shop doors, gave a nod of thanks to the sweeping shopkeeper, and took a gulp of root beer. Then another. He belched.

Fool glanced at him and stood.

"I know," Jack said.

It was time to meet his sister.

— 2 —

"It's you!"

Jack hadn't given much thought to where he might sleep tonight, but right off he knew he couldn't afford a place like this. The Astor House looked bigger than the funeral parlor in Kendall Plains. And that parlor, with its polished wood floors and red velvet curtains, had been the fanciest place Jack had ever seen.

Lumbering up the few wide porch steps, he entered the inviting glow of the hotel. Not as fancy as the funeral parlor, Jack decided, but he surely did enjoy the fireplace where he stopped to warm his hands. He wished he could bring Fool inside to get warm.

Approaching an older woman behind a shiny wood counter, Jack paused before speaking. He waited for the hurtful bugle noises from the fort to stop.

"Excuse me," Jack asked. "Does a girl . . . young lady . . . named Maggie Murphy work here?"

The black haired woman's words were as precise as her bun. She spoke without looking up.

"She'll be done on the hour and none the sooner."

Fool barked from outside and Jack hushed him. Jack sat in a straight–backed cane chair by the door where Fool could see him. An enormous grandfather clock graced the hallway. Jack chewed the fingernails on his right hand to pass the time. This clock ticked the slowest of any he'd known.

Ten minutes after it had chimed six times, a girl entered the lobby.

Sixteen–year–old Maggie wore a thick brown braid down her back, carried a folded white apron in one hand, and held a smile for the boy in the lobby. Hazel eyes and a pert nose distinguished her from Jack. But they shared high cheekbones, olive skin and a full mouth. A left dimple dug deep into her cheek when she smiled. Jack recognized it from the photograph of his father.

"Mrs. Bennett said you were looking for me?"

Jack thought her voice a blanket of spring flowers. In all the time he'd sat here, he hadn't decided what he should say when he met her. In fact, it hadn't even crossed his mind.

So he just stared at her.

Her smile flickered and her head tilted as she walked toward him, Jack capable only of following her with his eyes. Wondering if he should have gone to Boston. If he had done the right thing in coming here. If she would help him find the truth about his . . . their . . . father. If . . .

When she touched his chin and lifted his gaze to meet hers, her small gasp prickled his spine. He sat frozen. She covered her mouth and he watched in fixed awe as she looked into him as no living soul ever had.

Unable to move, Jack could only listen.

"Bird John," she whispered. "It's you."

~ ~ ~

Jack thought Maggie's room above Todd's and Bailey's Drug Store smaller than Pete's barn stall at home. It fit a bed, a stove, and a large trunk with a kerosene lamp that Maggie lit as soon as they entered. A pitcher, bowl and towel sat on top of a small table. Along with a photograph.

"You have her quiet nature," Maggie said.

She bent to jostle the fire in the small stove. Jack hadn't been able to take his eyes off the photograph since they'd arrived from the Astor House.

He'd tried for all his life to remember his mother. Tried to dream about her, but never could.

Maggie sat next to him on the bed. When he pulled away as she tried to smooth his hair, she folded her hands on her lap.

"I knew as soon as I saw you. The reddish hair." She smiled. "Your eyes."

Jack noticed the empty bin next to her stove and decided

he would buy her some coal tomorrow. He had some money left.

Dinner consisted of the last of her bread and cheese and from Jack's bag a large square of cornbread. When he expressed concern about eating the last of her food, she waved a hand at him and started untwisting her long braid, claiming she would be paid tomorrow so not to worry. Jack decided to buy her food tomorrow too, especially since he likely would be sharing it with her. At least for awhile.

He folded the small embroidered towel in which he'd carefully wrapped his cornbread.

"Is that your grandmother's?" she asked.

Jack hesitated, looking at the towel.

"Our grandmother's," she corrected herself quickly.

He stayed the growing heat in his belly.

"Yes." He stuffed the towel into his bag. "It was. She's dead."

Pronouncing his grandmother dead out loud spiraled the tight heat to his throat. Maggie shifted to face Jack's profile.

"How is it you're here on Mackinac, Jack?"

She'd asked him earlier but he hadn't answered her. Staring at the wall, it was some time before Jack spoke.

"Grandpa died in January. Not sure what from. He wasn't sick for long." He shrugged his shoulders and sighed. "He just died. Then right after . . . Grandma got sick." He picked at nothing on his knee. "She just wouldn't get up in the morning and then she . . . I cared for her the best I could and Doc Evans came and Mrs. Wenstrom from two farms over came every day but . . . "

Maggie touched his arm and he let its warmth rest.

"I was supposed to . . . " he touched the ticket stub in his pocket " . . . after they died . . . supposed to go to Boston. My . . . our Uncle Patrick and Aunt Sarah live there. He wanted me to apprentice to his carpentry business, but . . ." Jack's voice became a murmur. "I came here instead."

He thought of his grandmother's treasured St. Patrick rosary in his jacket pocket. The one she'd brought from Ireland. Maybe he should give it to Màggie.

His hand brushed the outside of his jacket pocket. He had taken it from his grandmother's nightstand before he left. Before a neighbor took it. Or it was put away. It held her touch. When Jack felt the cool smooth beads he knew the warmth of his grandmother's wrinkled hands. Could still smell her lavender scent on it. He shook his head if only to convince himself. No. His hand slid to his lap. He wasn't ready to give it up. Not even to Maggie. Not yet.

"Jack," Maggie said softly. "I'll tell you about our mother and . . . you tell me about our grandparents . . . and aunt and uncle and together . . . we'll know our family."

"What about our father?" His words were hushed like a secret. The tapestry of hurt in his eyes left Maggie momentarily speechless.

"I don't remember much but . . . " she began.

"They told me . . . my . . . our grandparents told me," Jack stuttered, "that he was killed in a military accident at Fort Mackinac. That . . ." his voice faded, "that he died saving another solder's life."

"I was around four," Maggie said. "All I knew was . . . " she rose, poking at the coal embers in hopes the fire might burn anew, " . . . I remember missing him."

Her laughter caught Jack off guard.

"He used to . . . " her arms swept upward with her voice, " . . . swing me high toward the sky and make me laugh." She stood still for a moment. Jack thought her willow tree graceful. "I remember that."

With sudden clarity, Jack realized he was not the only one hurting.

"Did anyone ever . . . find a . . . him . . . ?"

"No. He just never came home." Pulling her shawl tighter around her shoulders, she sat next to her brother. "How did you discover the truth?"

Jack started to face her but instead found comfort in petting Fool at his feet.

"When grandma was . . . dying . . . she told me. About our father leaving and . . . she told me she could never believe her son deserted his family. That in her heart she knew it was untrue." Jack paused with the memory. "She prayed for him and . . . asked for my forgiveness and . . . " he cleared his throat, "she told me about you."

A sad bugle call filled the quiet.

"You didn't know you had a sister?" Her voice rose to an awkward end with her question.

Finally, Jack looked at her.

"No."

In the lamplight's glow, a halo of light embraced Maggie.

"Poor Little Bird John," she whispered, shaking her head.

"Why do you call me that?"

Jack wondered if her smile belonged to their father or mother.

"That's what Mama called you."

"Why?"

"Your Ojibway name is . . . Bird John Punnichiace."

Jack swerved to face her, the shock of her words evident in his expression.

"It means New Born Bird," she said softly.

His brows furrowed, his head tilted with question.

"You didn't know this either?" she asked, her voice edged with awe.

"Know what?"

Rising, she retrieved the photograph of their mother, offering it to Jack.

"Our mother was Metis." She paused. "As are we."

Jack examined the framed photograph in his hand. The lovely young woman wore her dark hair in fashionable ringlets, her brown eyes danced above a high collared white blouse and dangling earrings. He thought her eyes shiny for him alone.

"What does that mean? Metis?"

Maggie sat with him.

"It's quite common." Inhaling deeply, her eyes connected with his. "Our father was Irish . . . "

Jack nodded with impatience, wanting the rest.

". . . and our mother's name was Amelie Roy. It's French

because her papa was a French trapper. But our mother's mother was Ojibway . . . Indian."

The bed jostled beneath them with Jack's spit words.

"We're half–breeds?"

Looking at the photograph again, he saw a woman like any woman he might have met in Ohio. Except for her coloring, she didn't look Indian. Not the way he thought of it. Maggie read his thoughts through his eyes.

"Mama worked as a fort laundress," she said. "That's how she met Papa."

Before Jack had felt proud to be the grandson of Michael and Bridget Murphy. Now he didn't know who he was anymore.

She watched him in vain for a sign of understanding. "It's a mixture–through marriage–of different people. Cultures." She waited. "We're Metis," she said, adding quickly, "Many here are."

Maggie detached her eyes from his and continued, her tone kind yet determined.

"Our mother died when I was five and . . . you were barely three. Cholera took her along with many others." Her eyes instructed Jack to pay attention. "She made sure we were well tended far away in the woods with the other children." Maggie smiled sad with memory. "She was so afraid you would get ill. You were so little. She . . . she asked often about her Little Bird." Maggie paused. "I remember."

Jack looked away. Maggie spoke slow and low.

"I was raised by our mother's tribe until I came to work

in Mackinac Village a few years ago."

Forearms on his legs, Jack's hands and head hung. It didn't make sense to him. Maggie folded her chilled legs beneath her on the bed. A mere glow peeked from within the stove.

"I'm not sure how your . . . our grandparents learned of our mother's death, but they did. And they came."

"How did we become separated?" he asked.

All his life he'd thought himself an only child. His father a hero.

"I had a broken leg and travel would have been too hard for me."

Jack's look of disbelief tore at her heart.

"I think . . . I'm sure they planned to come back for me, Jack. But it's . . . " she tried to follow his face as he turned from her, " . . . such a long way. And they knew I was well taken care of. You were a boy and . . . ."

His grandparents had lied to him. All his life. He barely found the words.

"They should have told me."

When he finally faced her, his voice cracked, his eyes blazed like blue fireballs.

"I would have made them come for you."

"Jack . . . "

He stood, facing her delicate beauty as she looked up at him.

"There's something I know," he said, sounding more like a man than a boy. He jabbed at his chest with his thumb as he spoke.

"My father would never have deserted his family. Or his duty. He would never . . . " he stopped to stay his tears, " . . . have left us. Never have let our mother die or us be separated. He . . . " Jack cleared his throat, lowered his rising voice, and straightened his shoulders before continuing. "I'm going to prove our father loved us, that he was a good man . . . and didn't desert anyone."

Before Maggie could say anything, Jack announced he was taking Fool for a last evening walk, the door thudding behind him.

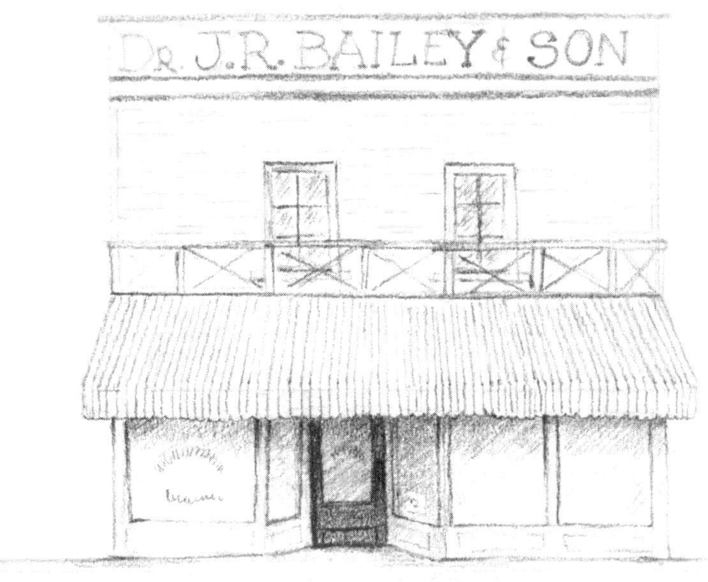

— 3 —

"A hungry dog and his boy"

Jack sat up with the fervor of an awakening turtle, trying to ignore the stiffness in his back from sleeping on the floor with his shoulder bag as a pillow and Fool's furry body for warmth. His head shook with wonder.

Here he sat in his sister's room on Mackinac Island.

His birthplace.

A muffled bugle from the fort reminded Jack of his plans.

First he spent a goodly sum of money on a bucket of coal and food items for his sister. He wasn't sure if she liked beans or beef jerky, but they had been cheap and kept well so he figured he should buy them. Jack glanced at his small, shabby surroundings. Maggie didn't seem like a fussy person. Hopefully she would want to go with him when he went to live in Boston with their Uncle Patrick and Aunt Sarah. Once he found the truth about their father–cleared his name–Jack planned to move on.

He'd decided to wait awhile before discussing that with her.

There was nothing for him here on this island. Except Maggie. And he hoped to talk her into going to Boston with him.

It struck him that his aunt and uncle might not know they had another niece. But he was sure they would welcome her. She was part of the Murphy clan. Family.

Jack's stomach gurgled so he grabbed a piece of jerky to eat on his way up to Fort Mackinac.

Two women, the youngest wearing a pale blue dress, one hand holding her skirt up off the dusty street, walked by Jack. A group of noisy soldiers on their way from the fort passed him in a large wagon. A carriage with a driver and three empty seats behind him turned off to Market Street.

Fool barked and chased after one particularly fancy black rig.

The harbor seemed busier than the village. A huge passenger steamship dwarfed sailboats and rowboats as they traveled to and from the piers and shore. The enormity of blue sky and lake–where blue met blue– made Jack feel as though he were at the earth's edge. Like he could just sail away into a blue foreverness.

He couldn't help but wonder if that was what heaven was like.

Maggie had warned him everything would become busier than bees in a rose garden once more tourists started arriving with the warmer weather.

Below Fort Mackinac sat a great fenced area enclosing a few small buildings. Jack immediately knew it was a garden from the uneven rows left over from the previous year's tending. Somehow it made him feel comfortable. Maybe, he thought as he started to trudge up the steep walk to the fort entrance, he could at least enjoy watching things grow again.

A tiny sparrow chirped and hopped in fine spring fashion on the walk in front of him. It had to be near 60 degrees today. And here it had been snowing yesterday. Jack shrugged.

This Michigan weather was surely strange.

The whitewashed fort walls glistened in the sunshine, smoke billowed from the buildings within. He noticed soldiers dressed in dark blue uniforms similar to the one his father wore in the photograph, rifles resting on their shoulders.

It was about half past nine when Jack stepped through a large archway into Fort Mackinac. A weak tinny bugle sounded. He watched as one set of eight soldiers marched across a large gravel area. One soldier yelled an order and eight soldiers changed places in a rapid, practiced manner with the other eight soldiers. Jack liked their shiny black boots. Fool sat and watched.

When they were done, Jack approached the soldier who had seemed in charge and had the most stripes on his sleeve.

"Sir?"

The man's thick mustache almost hid his mouth. He patted Fool's head and looked around.

"Your folks with you, Boy?"

"No, Sir. I'm . . . just my dog," Jack said.

It was harder to say than he had thought it would be. "Sir, do you know where I might find information about a soldier who served here a long time ago?"

The soldier rubbed his chin and stooped to pet Fool again. "Well, I don't know much about that, but maybe someone over in Post Headquarters can help you out. I'm First Sergeant Connors," he said. "Come with me."

Fool and Jack followed him a short walk to a wood building next to two other small buildings. Jack noticed soldiers walking to and from the many buildings that formed the perimeter around a great gravel parade ground. Three small white block buildings spanned the fort walls at regular intervals. He felt like he stood within another village.

Inside the Post Headquarters, Jack had to squint a few minutes until his eyes adjusted to the dim interior. A young mustached soldier sat at one desk writing. Another desk was hardly visible with all its piles of neatly stacked papers. An open doorway lead to another room which Jack couldn't see into.

The first sergeant exchanged salutes with the soldier behind the desk who was introduced as the adjutant, Lieutenant Marshall.

"This boy says," began First Sergeant Connors, "he's lookin' for a soldier from . . . how long ago did you say, boy?"

"I think it was 1874." Jack knew from Maggie that was when his father had left.

Fool barked from the porch and Jack shushed him. The

Adjutant's smile showed under his mustache.

"Well, Letters of Correspondence might give you some information," he said. "Can't promise you'll find what you're looking for. You got time to look through some letters, young man?"

"Yes, Sir," Jack said. Trying not to feel excited, he took a deep breath. "I've got time."

First Sergeant Connors left and Lieutenant Marshall set Jack up at the empty desk with a large folder. The folder bulged with letters filled with handwriting of various sizes and clarity– some had all printed words, some cursive, some large and loopy and some tiny bird scratch scrawls.

The lieutenant told Jack these were the Letters of Correspondence for Company F, 1st Infantry of Fort Mackinac from 1873 through 1875. Jack couldn't imagine how long it might take him to read through the thick pile. So he decided to just scan them for his father's name.

He was well into the second hour, his eyes starting to blur, when he saw it. Sean Murphy. On December 17, 1874, the post commander, Major Alfred Hough, wrote, "Private Murphy's apparent desertion is a mystery to me. He was an excellent soldier as demonstrated by his industry, intelligence and dedication to duty. He lived happily with his wife and children and seemed content. I can not fathom any reason why he would desert."

A quiet fire rose from Jack's belly, warming his face. Straightening his shoulders, he nodded to himself. He was right. His grandma was right. His father had no reason to leave his military duty or his family. No reason.

Jack neatly placed the letters back in the folder.

"Obliged, Sir," Jack said, turning to leave.

The lieutenant put down his pen. "Did you find what you were looking for?"

Jack glanced at him over his shoulder. "Some."

Fool's tail thumped the porch like a hard wind whips a full sail when he saw Jack walking his way.

"That dog of yours looks like he could use some food," the lieutenant said, gesturing at Fool in the doorway.

"He's fine," Jack said, scratching Fool behind the ears.

Jack didn't want to be beholden to anyone. After all, once he restored his father's good name, he would be leaving. He pet Fool. 'Skin and bones' is what his grandma would have called Fool. Poor dog hadn't had much more than bread to eat since they'd left Ohio.

Noticing that Jack hadn't left yet, the lieutenant added, "I'll bet Dutch could find some meaty scraps for him in the kitchen."

Jack guessed getting some food for Fool wouldn't make him beholden to anyone. Feeding a dog was different than feeding a person. Dogs didn't owe anybody anything.

"Thank you, Sir," he said.

Jack and Fool followed a Corporal Seth Anders into a long two story building kitty-corner from Headquarters.

Jack thought the corporal who wore his forage cap at a jaunty angle couldn't be too much older than him. Walking through a hallway to the back, Jack smelled food. By Fool's antsy behavior, Jack figured Fool did too.

"Hey Dutch," Corporal Anders greeted the short, balding, burly man wearing a white apron tied in front.

The cook reminded Jack of the Humpty Dumpty character from his old nursery rhyme book.

The corporal grabbed a carrot from an enormous green bowl on the table. Dutch slapped at his hand with a wooden spoon.

"What you got here?" Dutch asked, pointing at Fool.

Two twenty-foot long wooden tables groaning with large and small silver pots and pans stood across from each other. One soldier peeled carrots and potatoes while another stirred a steaming pot on a stove. Floor to ceiling shelves boasted glass jars and tin cans of various colors and sizes. More pots and pans hung from the ceiling, the breeze from the open back door swaying and lightly banging them together like out of tune wind chimes.

"Dutch, you got any leftovers for a hungry dog and his boy?" asked Corporal Anders.

Within what seemed like seconds, Fool lay next to a stove chewing on a meaty bone. Jack found himself sitting on a stool at one of the tables eating oatmeal with a dollop of honey. Dutch had insisted every growing boy needed oatmeal for breakfast when he'd plopped the steaming bowl in front of him. As Jack wolfed down his first hot food in days, Corporal Anders munched on a carrot and told him he had been instructed to take Jack to a soldier who had been at the fort for many years.

Someone who might have known his father.

— 4 —

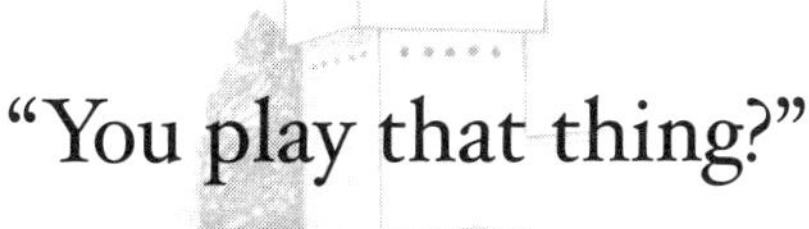

"You play that thing?"

"You play that thing?"

Jack shifted the fiddle on his back. He hadn't felt comfortable leaving it in Maggie's room.

"Some," he said.

Commissary Sergeant MacDougal's sideburns and mustache were as thick as his Scottish accent. His forage cap sat back on his sandy gray hair.

"To answer your question, Lad . . ." Sergeant MacDougal leaned back in his desk chair. "I do remember your father."

Jack's heart fluttered and settled.

"I didn't know him well, mind you." The sergeant's chair squeaked as he sat up. He folded his hands on the desk in thought. "Son, do you mind if we talk man to man?"

Standing in front of the sergeant's desk, Jack nodded, his thoughts raging with fear. Would Sergeant MacDougal tell him that his father was a ne'er do well? Or a scoundrel?

"You want to sit?" offered the sergeant, gesturing to a chair next to his desk.

"No thank you, Sir."

"Son, it's not uncommon for men to desert the fort here." He shrugged his shoulders and his hat fell further back. "Army life isn't for everyone."

Noting the confusion in Jack's eyes, Sergeant MacDougal continued. "Now, I'm not saying your father deserted for sure. Not if you think you know otherwise." He paused. "I didn't know Sean Murphy well enough to make a call about that." His hands opened and closed as he spoke. "I'm just saying, if he did desert . . . it doesn't mean he wasn't a good man in many ways."

Two soldiers entered the Commissary carrying large bulging bags over their hunched shoulders. One stopped to have Sergeant MacDougal sign a paper on a clipboard before following the other soldier into a room. The soldiers stopped to pet Fool on their way out since they had to step over him in the open doorway.

"Potatoes," Sergeant MacDougal said, his thumb jerking toward the storeroom where the soldiers had left their bags. "Can never have too many potatoes around here. Pretty soon we'll be growing our own again."

"I saw the garden." Jack wanted to steer the conversation back to his father but wasn't sure how.

"You good with growing things?"

Jack straightened his shoulders.

"I was a farmer in Ohio." Suddenly he felt much older

than fourteen. And he couldn't help but think how proud his grandpa would be of what he'd just said.

Sergeant MacDougal sat back in his squeaking chair, his eyes twinkling.

"You told me you just came here from Ohio?"

"Yes, Sir."

"With your mother?"

"No, Sir. I'm . . ." He spoke with an even determination. "I take care of myself now." Jack seized the opportunity. "Did you, might you have known . . . my mother, Sir? She was the fort laundress when my father served."

The sergeant's eyes squeezed into slits and his tongue wet his lips as he searched his memory. "Had a French name . . . "

Jack nodded. "Amelie."

"Aye, I do remember her somewhat." The sergeant smiled. "She was a pretty little lass. Used to hum when she worked." His smile faded. "She's gone?"

"Yes, Sir."

A tinny off-key bugle sounded. Sergeant MacDougal closed his eyes, shaking his head hard.

"You say you play that fiddle?" He waved a hand at Jack's back.

"Some."

"Well, some's better than none. You ever play a bugle, Lad?" the sergeant asked in one swoosh of question.

"No, Sir."

The hurtful bugle invaded the air again. Sergeant

MacDougal cringed.

"You want to learn?"

Jack could hardly believe it when he looked in the mirror.

He wore a soldier's uniform. Just like his father.

It surely wasn't anything he thought would happen when he'd come to the fort this morning. He shook his head in disbelief as he recounted the last few hours.

After listening to the fort musician mangle another military command, Sergeant MacDougal had hustled Jack next door to the Post Headquarters. He kept talking about how a man on his own in the world would do well to join the military. How if Jack could play the fiddle he carried on his back, no doubt he could learn how to play a bugle in no time. Their current musician had been pressed into service with the hopes he could learn to perform the required calls. But the fort was desperate for another musician.

And he thought it might be nice to have a musician who could actually play music for a change.

Jack's thoughts reeled. He only planned on staying until summer's end. Or until he could clear his father's name.

Would he be lying if he didn't tell them? And when the sergeant had stated that Jack looked like a 'strong strapping lad of sixteen years or more," Jack hadn't corrected him.

Jack decided he needed to find a confessional first chance he got.

It was when the sergeant had spoken of a place to stay, three meals a day, thirteen dollars a month musician's pay when and if the paymaster came every two months, and the chance to explore where his father used to serve, that Jack listened. Maybe by living in the fort he could find out what he needed to know about his father. Maybe he would run into a soldier that had spent time with his father. Or find a document that explained why his father had left. Maybe.

And, Sergeant MacDougal had added with a gleam in his eye, he could see to it that Jack worked in the garden as his fatigue duty earning thirty-five cents a day of extra duty pay.

The sergeant's brogue thickened the more animated he became. He had continued, slapping Jack's shoulders, his mouth barely visible beneath his mustache as he both begged and promised. Fool could stay in the kitchen with Dutch keeping the rats at bay while eating like a king, he'd said. Jack could see him throughout the day between duties and in the evening.

Jack had considered the burden he would be on Maggie, eating her food and staying at her place. Although he had planned to earn money by playing his fiddle on street corners and in saloons. Especially when all the tourists Maggie had talked about arrived.

Because Jack could fiddle.

In fact, Jack could play almost any instrument that had ever crossed his path.

Time after time as Jack was growing up, his grandparents were amazed at his innate musical ability. They couldn't imagine where he had inherited it from within the family.

No family member they knew could play music like Jack. Feel the music like him. Become one with it.

Never had Jack received a music lesson. He didn't even know how to read music. Yet if someone placed a guitar in his hands, he could make it sing. It was the same with a banjo. Or if he sat down at a piano.

His grandmother had said it was how God meant Jack to express himself since he had never been one to talk much.

The next few hours had been spent filling out paperwork and getting his uniform and supplies from the post quartermaster. He was fitted for a fatigue shirt, woolen trousers, a forage cap and leather boots. He truly appreciated the boots as he'd been stuffing his old ones with newspaper as of late. And he was given four pair of socks and new undergarments. Jack was sure his grandma would have been glad of those. The quartermaster's assistant told Jack he wouldn't be issued a dress uniform or rifle just yet.

That suited Jack just fine as he wasn't looking forward to wearing a spike on his head and had no earthly use for a rifle.

Yet here he stood. Looking at himself in a mirror.

Jack Michael Murphy was a soldier. Musician Murphy of Company E, twenty-third Regiment of Infantry.

"Musician Murphy," a voice came from behind.

Corporal Seth Anders appeared in the mirror's reflection. The thinnest person Jack had ever seen stood next to the corporal. Jack thought he looked like the scarecrow Grandpa had used last summer to keep crows off the crops.

"Musician Murphy, this is Private Wade Hockley. He's been serving as our . . . uh . . . musician . . . lately. You two will be spending a good deal of time together so I thought perhaps you should eat together at dinner tonight. Get to know each other a bit."

At the word 'dinner,' Jack felt a twang of panic.

"Uh, nice to meet you, Private Hockley," he said, shaking the private's boney hand.

Jack faced the corporal.

"Excuse me, Sir, but . . . uh . . . Captain Brady said I might have this evening to myself as I have some . . . private matters . . . in the village to attend to."

Corporal Anders smirked.

"A girl, right?" He dug his elbow into Private Hockley's skeleton frame. "I do believe Murphy has a girl in the village."

Jack sighed. He closed his eyes with dread.

"Yes, Sir. It's about a girl."

— 5 —

"You play baseball, Boy?"

Shades of apricot, lavender and cotton candy pink layered softly across the evening sky where it met the lake. Never had Jack seen so much blue at one time until coming to this island. Standing high above the village just outside the fort, he was sure he saw a bald eagle soar across the harbor above squawking seagulls. The waning sun sparkled like diamonds scattered across the lake. A soft buttery glow drifted lazy and warm across village roof tops until the lake swallowed the sun. The *City of Cleveland* passenger steamship whistled of its departure from Arnold Transit Docks.

On his walk down to the village, Jack looked the garden over. The ground looked hard, but there was work to be done. A carriage jingled by and Jack was glad he'd left Fool in the fort kitchen.

Fool needed to get used to the carriages.

The carriage horse made Jack think of Pete. He wondered if the old horse was doing well. Then his thoughts followed to his aunt and uncle. He wondered if they would be angry when they received his letter. Sergeant MacDougal had promised to mail it for him. Jack hadn't wanted to worry his aunt and uncle. They would be expecting him on the train in Boston within the week.

But he was on Mackinac Island. And it was his sister not his aunt and uncle that concerned him at the moment.

On his way to Astor House, Jack held an imaginary conversation with his sister. In this conversation, Maggie was happy that he would be staying at the fort instead of with her. And she wouldn't be upset that he planned on leaving by summer's end.

He chewed a fingernail on his left hand before stuffing his hand in his pocket, determined to stop his bad habit like he'd promised his grandmother.

His right hand found its way to his mouth.

Jack only had to wait a few minutes for Maggie outside Astor House before she appeared with a pretty blonde girl about her age. Maggie's long thick braid swatted her back as she tilted her head, her laughter skittering like a spring brook over stones.

Her smile tugged at Jack.

"Jack! You're here!" she almost yelled, skipping over to him like a school girl. The pretty blond followed.

"Inga," Maggie began. She spoke in a formal tone, taking Jack's hand in hers.

"This is my brother, Jack." Her sly smile suggested she had spoken of Jack to Inga. "Jack, this is my friend Inga. We work together."

Jack mumbled a greeting while almost looking Inga in the eye.

"We have to go," he told Maggie.

"Well, since Inga's here I thought maybe we could. . ."

"I need to talk to you."

Sighing disgust at her brother's ill manners, Maggie excused them from Inga and promised to do something with her the following night. Inga smiled at Jack before leaving. Jack didn't notice.

"Inga's Swedish," Maggie said as they walked down Water Street.

Jack walked a few feet in front of Maggie. She gathered her skirt every few seconds so she could run to catch up with him, her petite black boots trotting twenty tiny steps to ten of his strides.

"Her nose is too small," Jack said without slowing down.

Maggie erupted with laughter. "No it's not! It's. . .cute. Don't you think she's cute?"

"I bought you some coal and groceries today."

"You didn't have to do that," Maggie said. She rifled through her pocket withdrawing several coins. "I got paid today."

"Where do you want to eat dinner?" he asked.

She caught up with him again.

"Well, you said you bought. . ."

"No," he said. He stopped and she stopped beside him,

sighing her relief. "I'm taking you out to eat."

Maggie's eyes widened with smile. "Really? Why?"

Hands shoved in his pockets, Jack walked. "Where do you want to eat tonight?"

Maggie started trotting.

Maggie had never eaten in the dining room of the Palmer House before. Jack told her she could order anything she wanted. After all, he thought, he wouldn't be having any expenses for the next couple months. And she might take to what he had to say better on a full stomach.

He wasn't sure. He'd never had a sister before.

They'd almost finished their whitefish and mashed potatoes when Jack figured he should say something.

"So. . .I got a job today." He broke the last dinner roll in half.

Maggie's mashed potato filled fork halted half way to her mouth. "You did?" She smiled small. "Doing what?"

Buttering his roll, he snagged a small bite. "Playing music."

She seemed pleased until he told her where he would be playing music. And living.

"But. . .I thought you would be staying with me."

Jack wasn't used to dealing with wounded feelings. Especially in girls.

"It. . . you'll have your privacy and I won't have to eat

your food," he said, thinking that sufficient explanation.

Her fork clanked onto her plate.

"I thought we would be able to spend time together. But if you're living and working at the fort. . ."

He recognized her pout. Becky Evans at school had done that for days after he hadn't sat with her at a school picnic once. Jack didn't think this was a good time to tell Maggie he wasn't planning to stay on the island past summer.

After she refused dessert, Jack pretty sure it was only to make him feel badly, they walked down the street to the point. The evening air had turned bone-chilling damp. He was glad he'd bought Maggie more coal. He pointed to a land mass across the lake outlined like a rock in the night.

"What's that?" he asked.

"Round Island," she said.

He tried and failed to skip a stone across the water.

"Does anybody live there?"

"No," she said. "They get firewood from there and. . . sometimes people go picnicking there."

She skipped one stone three times.

Waves rushed to and from the rocky shore in a quiet song. Frogs galumphed softly in the distance.

"You know," he began, "there are two of us . . . musicians . . . so I can get time off. And Sundays are mostly free time."

Maggie plucked at her shawl.

"I don't work every Sunday," she muttered.

He couldn't be sure in the dark, but Jack thought she smiled.

"You can go on a picnic with me maybe next Sunday," she said.

Jack thought for a moment. "Well, I guess I can. . ."

"With me and Inga and Daniel. . ."

Jack's whistle sounded like a deflating balloon. Failing to skip another stone, he shook his head. And feared if he argued he might end up at a dance which would be twice as bad as a picnic.

A steamship with small lights outlining its deck passed them on its way out of the harbor.

"Somebody's leaving," Jack said.

He couldn't see the shine in her eyes as she looked up at him. "As long as it's not you."

Minutes passed before he spoke.

"What time on Sunday?"

Jack spent as much time as he dared visiting Maggie knowing he would be up before dawn the next morning. *Just like on the farm*, he told himself.

Fort Mackinac looked like a castle from below at night with light cascading from its outdoor lanterns and windows. Jack was almost to the entryway when he heard the call: "All's well." The sentry asked him for the password. He remembered it from Corporal Anders telling him earlier.

Supper was done so Jack decided to visit Fool in the

kitchen. Fool lay by a stove, a large meatless bone beside him. He almost knocked Jack over with his greeting. After letting Fool outside one more time for the night, Jack told him to stay and be a good boy and walked down the hallway to his area of the barracks.

"Hey, Murphy!" Corporal Anders hailed him from the entryway.

Jack felt glad to see someone he recognized.

"So," the corporal began, "did you. . .uh. . .take care of that. . .situation. . .in the village?"

Jack nodded, forcing himself to smile. He was more tired than during harvest season and he'd hardly done a lick of work all day.

"I'm supposed to help you get settled in," said the corporal.

He ushered Jack through a wash room area into the main barracks.

The soldiers' barracks was a square wood-paneled room with a few large wooden tables in the middle. A kerosene lamp glowed on each table. Cots lined the walls on either side of the tables. Jack's bag and fiddle had been placed on a middle cot, a small storage chest at its base. Somehow leaving his fiddle here didn't worry him.

Two men played and one man watched a game of checkers at a middle table. Another man lay on his cot reading a magazine while six men were playing a rather rowdy game of cards across the room. One man sitting next to a pot-bellied stove played the harmonica. Jack noticed all eyes had landed on him when he and the corporal entered.

The corporal told Jack the men would get around to introducing themselves. Jack realized all the men were privates just about the time he realized he'd had his own bedroom his entire life and how strange it would feel to sleep in the same room with all these older men.

At least the cot springs and thick cotton stuffed mattresses were likely to be a good deal more comfortable than Maggie's cold wooden floor.

He was told the location of the latrine, mess hall at the back of the building, and shown his kit of soap and toiletries, including a razor and shaving cream. When the corporal introduced Jack as the new musician, the men exploded in a raucous round of applause.

An older stocky soldier approached and stood in front of Jack, feet apart, arms akimbo.

"No doubt we need better bugling 'round here," the soldier said. "But I got an important question."

The room had become silent: all eyes rested on Jack.

"You play baseball, Boy?"

6

"Soldier boy Jack"

Clinging to a small boat in a storm, dark waves washed over him, pulled at him. He screamed and screamed a voiceless scream. A sound. Was someone coming to save him? But it never got closer. A voice floated, soothed. Just as he was sure he was going down for the last time, the bucking edge of the boat slipping from his grasp, his surroundings turning gray, Jack awoke, sweaty and shaking.

To a thickly mustached, wild-haired man in baggy underwear standing over him. The man was telling Jack to wake up or he'd miss Assembly and there would be hell to pay.

Jack realized the sound he'd heard in his nightmare was Private Hockley sounding Reveille. And Jack was pretty sure Private Wade Hockley's bugle playing wasn't likely to save him from anything.

The other way around was more likely.

Pulling on his boots, he wondered. Had he heard a

voice in his dream? He hadn't recognized it. But it had made him feel better somehow.

On his first day as a soldier, Jack thought more information than he had learned in all his fourteen years had been thrown his way.

After Reveille, the men had five minutes to assemble on the parade ground in front of the barracks. Jack just tried to do what everyone else was doing. He stood at attention and kept his chin up. The first sergeant took roll call. Then Jack followed his new comrades to the wash room. They walked to the back of the barracks mess hall for breakfast. Before pounding down broiled bacon, bread, beef hash, and potato hash, Jack sneaked into the kitchen. He found Fool happily in the midst of his own breakfast.

"He goot dog, you Fool," Dutch praised before yelling at a soldier wearing a grease–covered apron to make more coffee.

Corporal Anders showed Jack around the fort while Private Hockley tended to the musician duties. Jack was getting the hang of standing at attention. He struggled with remembering to salute officers. He was already familiar with the Post Commissary, Headquarters and the Quartermaster's Storehouse. These buildings stood in a row across from the South Sally Port entrance. Jack had been told this was the entrance Captain Brady wanted all his men to use.

Jack was shown inside the guardhouse where two soldiers who had been charged with drunk and disorderly conduct played cards in the cell room. Corporal Anders explained they were awaiting a garrison court martial. Listening to them laugh, Jack didn't think they felt too badly about it.

The corporal walked Jack around the inside of the fort. He pointed out the schoolhouse that was not currently in use. The officers' children attended the village school. He showed Jack the Officers' Stone Quarters at the front of the fort, remarking that it was over a hundred years old and had been built by the British. On a hill above the parade ground were three officers' houses with broad porches. These four structures were where the officers lived with their families, the corporal finished.

Jack had noticed a little boy rolling a hoop with a stick earlier near the Officers' Stone Quarters.

"The officers have parties like nothing you've seen," the corporal said. "That Lieutenant Pratt's wife, Kate, can play the piano as pretty as I ever heard," he added.

As they walked around the fort, Jack saw more than working soldiers. A well-dressed couple and their small children strolled across the parade ground. Two young ladies, parasols twirling overhead, headed toward the gun platforms. When asked about their presence, Corporal Anders sighed.

"Tourists," he said. "This is nothing. Wait until the weather gets warmer. They'll be everywhere."

"But don't they. . ." Jack began.

The corporal stopped. "Captain Brady has given orders we are to be kind and courteous and. . . helpful. . ." he rolled his eyes at these last words, ". . .to the tourists who like to roam the fort."

The tour ended with the fort hospital outside the east fort walls. Corporal Anders explained that an old fort hospital at the west side of the parade ground now served as a storehouse for quartermaster supplies.

"What about those little houses along the fort walk?" asked Jack. He pointed to the small square buildings.

"Blockhouses, Murphy. They used to be for sentries to use looking for the enemy." The corporal laughed with his last words. "But now they hold a water tank, ordnance supplies and one's a paint shop."

Corporal Anders slapped Jack on the shoulder.

"You'll learn it all, day by day."

Jack was sure he wouldn't be here long enough to learn half of what he was supposed to know. And he didn't even know any of the bugle calls yet.

A bugle filled the air with what sounded like wounded bear moans. Jack figured if it had been a real bear, it would have been a goner.

"First Sergeant's Call," said the corporal. "Sergeant MacDougal wanted you to stop by to see him before Recall from Fatigue."

"What's. . . when's Recall from Fatigue?" asked Jack, nibbling on an index finger.

"It's right before Dinner Call."

Blowing his cheeks full with frustration, Jack realized Corporal Anders was teasing him when the corporal smiled and said, "You've got about half an hour."

Sergeant MacDougal had winked when he told Jack

that he had arranged for gardening to be Jack's fatigue duty. Corporal Wickes had overseen it all last year but, the sergeant had sighed, his enlistment was up and he married a local girl and took off for Chicago last fall.

When Jack had asked about learning his music, the sergeant explained until the garden soil could be tilled, Jack would spend time with Private Hockley learning the military calls. Once the garden could be worked, Jack would spend his early mornings working there and the rest of his day learning, and hopefully teaching, the bugle calls.

The month of May blossomed on Mackinac Island with the sweet innocence of a young girl donning an Easter bonnet. Purple crocus and cheerful daffodils outside Dutch's kitchen reached for the sun. Bird chatter started earlier every morning. Each day tree buds grew fatter, preparing to burst open like school doors the day before summer vacation. Each day the sun felt warmer on Jack's face as he sat with Private Hockley learning the bugle.

When Private Hockley first explained that fort musicians had to know over twenty different calls, Jack felt like resigning.

But learn them Jack did. Private Hockley would play his version of Reveille, and Jack would play the right version of Reveille. It went like that all the way down the list of calls. Then the private asked him if he could play the fife. Jack said he doubted it and Private Hockley said he didn't doubt it. So when Jack was presented with a small fife that had been locked away because nobody could play it, he tried it. He didn't take to it right away like he had the bugle. In no time he could play a decent tune.

They practiced on the headquarters porch. After a while, the adjutant asked them nicely to go behind the fort and practice. He knew where they were if they were needed. Jack liked this. That meant time with Fool. Dutch kept the kitchen door at the back of the barracks open during decent weather.

When Jack was asked if he knew how to shoot a rifle, he said he'd hunted every fall with his grandpa. He'd shot, cleaned and dressed a buck before. He could skin a rabbit. But neither was his favorite thing to do. His family had hunted for food and, unless it was necessary, he'd rather not shoot anything. Laughing, Corporal Anders said he figured it probably wouldn't be necessary unless they were attacked. The corporal had winked, telling Jack he should keep his trigger finger in working order, just in case.

Corporal Seth Anders had been a Fort Mackinac soldier for the last two of his nineteen years. He hailed from a small Illinois town, having joined the army for adventure. He'd only been a corporal for five months and was fairly proud of his achievement. Even though their sleeping quarters differed since the corporal was an officer, he and Jack spent a good deal of their off time together. Jack looked to him to answer his questions about military procedures. Corporal Anders always answered him in an easy fashion. He took Jack into the village and helped him open an account at Gallagher's Grocery where many soldiers had credit to make purchases between their long awaited paychecks.

At first, Jack didn't want to open an account. His grandpa had never been one to favor debt. And Jack planned on using his first paycheck to pay for his train ticket to Boston. But, Jack thought, if Maggie needed something, he could get it for her.

So he opened an account. Just in case.

Early on his third morning as a soldier, several of Jack's barracks mates took an interest in him.

"How old are you, Boy?"

Private Sondowski stood behind Jack with a shaving kit in hand.

Jack's voice rasped as he lowered it an octave. "Sixteen," he lied. He almost didn't recognize his own voice saying it. He wondered what the penance would be for telling the same lie twice.

"That right?" the burly private asked.

Jack looked away as he nodded. He didn't need to look at the private to realize this soldier didn't spend much time in the washroom.

"Well then," the private continued, "I'd say it's about time you started shaving."

Jack started to tell him he only had a little while before he had to play First Call, but the private wouldn't listen. A few more soldiers had awakened and were stepping into their pants, pulling up their suspenders.

Private Sondowski steered Jack in front of a small wall mirror and handed him the mug and brush. He leaned over Jack's shoulder. The private's breath might have inspired a snail to race. And win.

"Now, make sure you mix that shaving cream up good, Boy," said the private, his hand whipping an invisible mug for demonstration, "or your razor won't pull right."

For some reason, several soldiers had taken a keen interest in Jack's shaving ritual. They crowded around him like crows around a newly seeded garden.

The private poured a bit of water into the mug. Jack whipped it into lather with the shaving brush like he had watched his grandfather do so often.

"That's good, Boy," offered Private Norman. "Now, just lather it good on your face."

When Private Norman tried to slather it on Jack's face for him, Private Sondowski slapped his hand.

"I'll help the boy."

"But I have to. . ." Jack tried to speak.

A flock of soldiers had now invested their pre-Reveille moments in watching Jack shave.

In no time Jack understood his bunk mates' interest in 'helping' him shave.

Someone had added salt, sugar and flour to his mug so the lather stuck to his face like paste.

When Jack headed to the wash room, he left a room full of soldiers snorting with raucous laughter.

7

"Maggie May"

After sounding Call for Inspection 9:30 Sunday morning, Jack was free. He'd been worried about passing his first inspection, but Corporal Anders had helped him prepare.

Captain Brady had issued Jack a pass for the remainder of the day. Jack had promised Maggie he would go on a picnic with her. And her friends.

Morning brought mist and cool and an amazing assortment of chattering birds behind the barracks as Jack played with Fool. He'd missed Fool, but Jack felt good knowing he was well cared for and only a minute away anytime he wanted to pop in and see him. Dutch proudly announced he'd not seen one rat since Fool had been there. Then he filled Fool's dish by the fireplace with meat tidbits.

Part of Jack wanted the rainy weather to stay so he didn't have to go on the picnic. But he wanted to see Maggie. So when the sun replaced the clouds, Jack figured it was for the best. Although it confounded him that he and Maggie couldn't go on a picnic by themselves.

Around noon he met Maggie at Arnold Transit Docks on Water Street. Her pale yellow dress with white lace trim set off her dusky beauty. Shiny dark ringlets bounced about her face. A sweet clean fragrance told him she'd recently washed her hair. She looked older than the last time he'd seen her just a few days ago. Discovering arrangements had been made for a row boat, Jack dug into his pockets for money. Maggie gently stayed his hands, smiling, her face turning a soft shade of peach.

"Oh, don't worry about that, Jack." She almost floated as she spoke. "Daniel has taken care of the cost."

Jack stopped, hands still in his pockets. "That was...good of him."

As if pronouncing the name had summoned the person, a tall handsome blonde boy in his late teens bounded toward them. Jack watched Maggie's expression change from happy to angelic.

"Maggie May!" A jacket slung over one shoulder, Daniel stopped on a dime in front of Maggie.

"What did he call you?" asked Jack.

"Shhhhh, Jack."

Daniel reached for the handle of the large red and white cloth covered basket at Maggie's feet. Jack tried to beat him to it.

"All set!" Daniel announced.

Jack thought Daniel's teeth looked too big for his

mouth. Like a drawing he'd once seen of a walrus. A straw skimmer hat topped his close cropped yellow hair and he sported a barely visible pencil-thin mustache.

Jack rubbed his own naked upper lip. Maggie worked her way between the two boys.

"Daniel," she said. "I'd like you to meet my brother, Jack. Jack, this is Daniel Ishminking. He's in charge of the front desk at The Astor House."

Jack shook Daniel's extended hand for Maggie's sake.

When Maggie noted Jack's tight unrelenting grip, she interrupted. "Let's collect Inga."

They walked down the dock to the street: Maggie and Daniel. And Jack.

After meeting up with Inga, they made their way to a small dock where boats were rented. Daniel took charge, making a show of paying the fee and helping the ladies into the boat. Jack stepped in uneasily. After asking the girls' permission to roll up his shirtsleeves, Daniel rowed. Maggie made sure Jack and Inga sat next to each other in the rowboat. Jack enjoyed this view of Mackinac Island. The craggy bat caves, the tiny green buds dotting the trees, and the newly born scattering of multi-colored wildflowers along the island's edge entranced him. He enjoyed it as long as they stayed along the edge of the island.

Because Jack couldn't swim. And the memory of his nightmare remained strong.

Daniel decided they should picnic at Devil's Kitchen and then double back to visit Arch Rock. It was a beautiful day after all and they had the afternoon. He was sure Jack would enjoy both places. Maggie smiled at Daniel with appreciation of his thoughtfulness. But her eyes threw sharp poison darts at her brother. He just continued enjoying the view, watching that they didn't stray too far from shore.

And ignoring Inga.

They landed at Devil's Kitchen. As Jack helped Maggie spread a blanket in one of the shallow caves, he could tell she was upset. And he didn't think it was with her precious Daniel or Inga.

"What did I do?" he asked, trying to flap the blanket even on the uneven ground.

She smoothed the blanket without looking at him.

"Nothing," she said.

When she stood, her cheeks shone pink, her fierce eyes jabbing him from a distance. Jack took a step back.

"Absolutely nothing," she said. "*That's* what you did."

"What?" he asked, he arms opening with a plea of innocence.

Daniel was showing Inga a nearby cave.

"Shhhhh." Maggie waved at him. "Don't...say anything."

Jack just stood there afraid to move. Or speak. His sister could be downright scary.

"You're not talking to Inga at all," Maggie whispered

loudly. "You. . .you're ignoring her and that's very rude."

Jack thought for a moment.

"Why do I have to talk to her? She's your friend."

Maggie stared at him in a long moment of disgust before calling Inga and Daniel over for lunch.

For the rest of the afternoon, Jack tried to talk to Inga, but he didn't know what to say after they had discussed the weather. Maggie had told him to compliment Inga, but he didn't want to because then she would think he liked her.

They visited Arch Rock which Jack thought an amazing formation. Ohio had been nothing but flat and more flat. When Daniel climbed onto the middle of the arch, beckoning for Jack to join him, Jack chose to stay on the ground. He couldn't forget Daniel's snide smile as he hopped down, winking at him.

"Missed quite a view there, Jack-O," Daniel had said before slapping him on the back and whispering, "Maybe next time."

Jack insisted on rowing on their way back to the village. That way he didn't have to sit next to Inga and he could work out his anger on the oars. As much as he'd wanted to see Maggie today, he decided his afternoon would have been better spent with Fool. He preferred cleaning Pete's stall to this torture. Instead he had to watch Daniel and Maggie google-eye each other and Inga pout. He swallowed hard so as not to retch when Daniel sang a rousing rendition of "Oh My Darling Clementine," replacing the word 'Clementine' with 'Maggie May'.

Jack couldn't figure out why his sister didn't see Daniel

whatever-stupid-name for the no account mongrel that he so obviously was. And why she expected him to like a girl whose nose was too small.

That night the men tried to get Jack to play his fiddle but he wasn't in the mood. He thought they might have been trying to make amends for the shaving incident. But he wasn't really mad about it. Looking back, he supposed it was funny.

Lying in his cot in the dark, listening to Gus next to him snort like a cornered pig on market day, Jack guessed he was just feeling lonely.

Sometimes when he awoke in the morning, he still expected to smell his grandma's hotcakes. To hear Hank the rooster. To pull on his clothes and go out to the barn to milk Beulah and Kate. To see the sun spreading the pinkish yellow of day behind the barn weathervane.

To see his grandparents at the breakfast table.

When he closed his eyes he could still take himself there–taste the orange marmalade, the fresh warm milk. Smell the spicy kitchen smell. See his grandmother's blue egg-gathering basket she used every morning hanging by the green kitchen screen door his grandpa had made. Sometimes he could even hear that green door squeak before it clattered twice, finally closing with the solemn grace of an Amen.

But that was no more. It was all gone. His grandparents

were gone and the farm sat quiet. He hadn't been able to stay to see the auction of the farm equipment and household belongings. He couldn't bear to watch it.

So he'd packed a bag, called his dog, strapped on his fiddle and left. Just walked out the kitchen door knowing he was hearing it clatter closed for the last time.

And here he was.

Turning over in his cot, trying to get comfortable, Jack decided he needed to do what he had come to do. He'd already found his sister. And meeting Maggie had made him feel connected to his mother and father. It made what he had to do more important. He needed to regain his father's honor. It didn't seem important to Maggie.

Staring at the dim outline of a ceiling lamp, Jack sighed.

But it was important to him.

He lay still for a few seconds before throwing back his covers, stealing to the kitchen, and returning to finally find sleep with his hand enmeshed in a mass of soft golden fur.

— 8 —

"A place to stay"

It felt strange to Jack not to be wearing overalls when he tilled soil.

His superior officers had agreed Jack's farming skills were needed in the garden. So Private Hockley was scheduled to play First Call through Drill Call. Jack had the fort cows, Betty Lou and Pretty Girl, milked well before Reveille. Then, after Assembly and breakfast, he worked in the gardens until it was time to play Recall from Drill through Taps most days.

Snorting a laugh, he recalled how Maggie had worried that his being fort musician would keep him from sharing her company. But she was the one who was usually busy. With Daniel. Jack watched Fool chase birds in the cool morning mist. He hushed him from barking. At least he got to spend time with his dog in the early mornings.

Jack hacked at the dirt with increased vigor. Daniel whatever-his-name-was wasn't right for Maggie. It burned him when he thought of how she lit up like a firefly when telling him how Daniel had escorted her to a Mackinac Island Literary Society presentation the other evening. So what if he almost had a mustache.

It was important to get the garden planted as soon as possible. Northern Michigan had a short growing season. It wasn't like in Ohio where Grandma would have had her kitchen garden in a few weeks ago. Jack figured the island's last frost would likely be by month's end.

Jack didn't even mind his before breakfast milking chores. He liked the feel of his shoulder warm against the cow's heavy belly, the familiar ping of milk streaming into the metal bucket.

He almost expected to hear Grandma ring the porch bell to call him in for breakfast. Or hear Grandpa yell for him to get washed up claiming there'd be nothing but an empty plate left if he dawdled.

"Stop it, Fool dog!"

Jack tried to yell at Fool quietly. He didn't want to disrupt the pure peace that hovered about the early morning garden like an angel over a prayer. Cool gray mist greeted Jack and Fool every morning. Fool usually just dug or sniffed about, but this morning a squirrel had teased him and he wasn't about to have it.

Each morning Jack hoed and figured where the seeds should be planted for that day. He'd pretty much figured it out for the whole garden on a day to day schedule. But sometimes weather or lack of zeal by the soldiers working on it made him alter it.

After the final frost they'd plant beets, beans, onions, green corn, lettuce, cucumbers, parsnips, peas, radishes, squash, rutabagas and potatoes. Dutch said if they had a good harvest, he would bake a shoofly pie for everyone. A Pennsylvania Dutch creation he brought with him to Fort Mackinac, it had become a favorite of Sergeant MacDougal's. The sergeant claimed if they were ever attacked, they could place shoofly pies around the fort, miring the enemy in the molasses goo like a mule in a mud hole.

Maggie had been right about how Mackinac Island would change with the warmer weather.

Passenger steamships, yachts and sailboats shimmered in the harbor like stars on a clear night. The village was busier than a few weeks ago with tourists arriving from Chicago, Detroit, and beyond. Neighing horses and crying babies blended with seagull mews and steamship blasts.

It all reminded Jack of a glass jar full of brightly colored candies when he viewed it from the fort. Never had he seen so many fancy black carriages in one place. It had taken him a few minutes to cross Market Street on his way to visit Maggie a few days ago.

Dutch kept the door open to the grassy garden area behind the kitchen during the day. The kitchen held the heat from cooking. Only two small windows allowed light in and heat out. The open door allowed Fool to come and go as he pleased like at the farm. Dutch claimed he was going to train Fool to rabbit hunt. Then he could just send Fool off when he wanted a rabbit for stew. Jack laughed, claiming it really didn't work that way.

Jack took to military life. In many ways it reminded him of the routine of farm life. Rising early, doing chores, eating breakfast and then back to work. He liked rising before all the others and visiting Dutch in the kitchen. It took Jack awhile to get used to Dutch's accent and his kind of teasing. His humor differed from his grandpa's which had often been related to a lesson or homily.

Dutch was just plain silly. He named his favorite wooden mixing spoons Gustave and Mabel, refusing to let any soldier touch them upon pain of unending potato peeling duty.

He made Jack laugh.

Jack had even started drinking coffee. With some cream and sugar added. Dutch teased him that it was really the other way around.

When Jack walked into the kitchen early mornings, the crickets were still chirping their night song. Dawn's fresh coolness filled the air. Dutch had the stove glowing as plump piles of cloth-covered bread dough filled one table like little tin soldiers in a row.

Jack sometimes wondered if Dutch ever slept.

Dutch greeted him with, "Got you cup of hot milk ready, Boy."

Jack would sit across from him at a long wooden table, sip his coffee and play with Fool. Sometimes they'd talk.

Dutch had steered Jack to soldiers, some officers, who might have known his father. He'd told Jack some villagers he might talk to as well. Dutch always answered Jack's questions but he never asked any.

And sometimes they just kept each other company as early bird chatter and the rhythmic thudding of kneaded bread dough filled the quiet. Then Jack would gather his jacket and hat. He'd head down to milk the cows and work in his garden. His mornings started before the sun in the garden and ended in the evening with the sounding of Taps. In between, Jack practiced the fort calls and spent as much time working in the kitchen as he could to be close to Fool.

Often he sneaked Fool from the kitchen late at night, letting him sleep under his cot. Early the next morning he'd sneak him back to the kitchen. On these mornings, Dutch would pretend he didn't see Fool and Jack. He'd just keep kneading his thick hands into the soft dough and announce loudly to no one that he hadn't seen a varmint in weeks.

Then he'd wink at Jack and pour his 'cup of hot milk'.

As morning broke earlier and evenings lingered, in the midst of all the military order and regimen of the army, came baseball.

The Never Sweats was the name of the Fort Mackinac Base Ball Club.

When team members discovered Jack had played baseball with his school friends, he was invited to practice with them. Practices were Sunday afternoons and some evenings in good weather. They used the newly laid out diamond on the large parade ground behind the fort. Later each day, as spring drifted into summer, soldiers gathered for batting and pitching practice. Claiming Jack had the youngest legs and strongest back, they made him the practice catcher. Fool was given the honor of snagging fly balls in right field when Commander Brady's seventeen-year-old son, Griffin, was unavailable. Sometimes tourists riding or walking by waved or stopped to watch for awhile.

Lieutenant Edward Pratt was the team captain and second baseman. Knowing the young lieutenant had a young family to support, Jack was surprised when Pratt donated money to the team. His contribution of four dollars purchased two new bats at forty cents each, a real League baseball, three bases and a catcher's mask. Jack was most grateful when the mask arrived. The Never Sweats even played practice games against village teams. Practices were taken quite seriously as the honor of Fort Mackinac would soon be at stake. Come Fourth of July, the Never Sweats had a big game against the Diamond Baseball Club of Cheboygan. Jack hoped to play for the honor of Fort Mackinac.

Doc Bailey kept them all informed of what was going on in the world of baseball. He attended as many practices as he could. The good doctor looked strange standing among the well-to-do fans with his long thin beard and black hat.

Many a sprained ankle, bruised finger and sore elbow kept Doc Bailey's smelly ointments and wraps close by.

Everyone agreed that Private Wade Hockley's musical talents had improved. To tolerable. Evenings in the barracks meant games of whist and "Kingdom Coming" or "Oh Dem Golden Slippers" played on the harmonica. Jack also enjoyed playing chess or checkers or reading, but he wouldn't gamble.

He wouldn't gain debt. He knew that would make his grandfather proud.

When his barrack mates finally convinced Jack to play his fiddle the last Sunday evening in May, they were left with their mouths hanging open. Never had they seen someone so young play so well. Some said they had never seen anyone fiddle as well as young Murphy. As the busyness of the barracks settled into the still of night, the men just talked. Some spoke of Private Josh Windom being assigned to three months of hard labor for falling asleep on sentry duty. Some made plans to go fishing at Round Island to catch perch for Dutch. Others spoke of family and plans for the future.

It was as though this place was his home and these men his family. They looked out for each other. Respected each other. Playing on the baseball team here was so different from throwing the ball around a schoolyard with boys his age. He'd spent a good deal of time with Corporal Seth Anders when off duty. They'd explored and built fires in Skull Cave that the wind blew out. Even though he was a corporal, they were friends. And Sergeant MacDougal–or

Mac as he was called– came around or asked Jack to visit him in the Commissary.

Jack realized he wasn't chewing his nails as much.

He'd come to terms with the lies his grandparents had told him about his father and never telling him about Maggie. He knew they loved him and were just trying to protect him.

When he thought of them now it was with more good than bad: more with pleasure than pain. He'd lost them but found his sister. His aunt and uncle in Boston had telegraphed Jack. They hoped he would join them as soon as he could. Jack was to let them know if he needed anything.

Although so much had happened since he'd arrived barely a month ago, Jack finally felt a calm. Settled.

Like he belonged.

— 9 —

"Fiddle Dee Dee"

When Jack heard Doc Bailey needed someone to fill the matron position at the post hospital, he made sure Doc knew he had a sister who would be perfect for the position.

Jack wanted Maggie closer. She'd been spending too much time with that cad Daniel. This way Jack could spend more time with her for however long he might be staying. And she would make ten dollars a month which was more than she earned at the Astor House. He had even figured she could share a room in the village with the fort laundress.

Jack played Reveille with extra energy the morning he planned to tell her about her new job.

He'd found her at the Astor House while he was in the village picking up some supplies for Mac. First he'd spotted Inga, whose face turned pink as a peony when she saw him in the second floor hallway. When he'd asked where his sister was, Inga had sighed dreamily and pointed to a room two doors down.

"Jack." Maggie stopped dusting a table. "Is something wrong?"

"No, no." Jack spoke in a rush. "Listen, I don't have much time." He stood tall with pride as he made his announcement. "You'll be working at the post hospital from now on."

Maggie titled her head and smiled. "I'm what?"

"You can work at the post hospital now."

"I can what?" The feather duster fell to her side.

"You would make ten dollars a month. I could see you a lot more often before I. . .anyway. . ."

"Before you what. . .?"Maggie asked, her eyes slanted with question.

"Nothing. I just. . ." Stepping closer, he tucked a loose strand of hair back into her white lace maid cap. "Just . . . go to the post hospital tomorrow right after work. Doc Bailey will be there."

He waited for her to explode with excitement.

"What if I don't want a new job?"

"And you can share a place in the village with Ellie, the fort laundress. She's engaged to Corporal Marley."

Before she could blink, Jack disappeared.

"What if I don't want a new job?" she called after him down the hallway.

Maggie went to see Doc Bailey the next afternoon and she did get the job at the hospital. She would start the following week.

The same afternoon Jack had 'informed' her of her new job, Maggie received a gift.

A woman had returned to her hotel room as Maggie was cleaning it. The woman started to pack her assortment of lovely dresses. Her personal maid had taken ill and couldn't assist her. Maggie had offered to help. Turquoise, yellow and lavender hues scattered across the full skirted taffeta dresses: one dress shone a delicate summer rose pink.

When the woman tried to give Maggie money for her time, Maggie had smiled and said it was her pleasure to help. The woman had looked Maggie up and down.

"Then, my dear," the woman had said, "I want you to take this pink dress for your trouble."

Maggie had backed away from her. "Oh, no, Ma'am. I could never. . ."

"Tsk tsk, my dear." The woman had grabbed both Maggie's hands. "I haven't been able to wear this pink dress since my last child." She'd patted her waist and smiled. "And it looks to be a perfect fit for you. And a good color." Taking the dress from the top of the suitcase, she smoothed it over her arm. "Please. I don't know what I shall do with it if you don't take it."

"But I. . ."

"I thought perhaps," the woman had begun in a sly voice, "that you might have a young beau who would appreciate seeing you in this dress?"

Maggie had paused. The woman transferred the dress and a small matching purse to Maggie's arm before whispering, "Have a good time for me."

Within the fort and in the village below, Mackinac Island thrummed with life.

Tourists seemed to enjoy the evening dress parades at the fort best. Sometimes twenty or more people watched the ceremony. Children romped as their parents visited.

Ojibway Indians set up huts along the beach area to sell their hand-woven baskets, dolls, maple syrup and trinkets. The women wore patterned blouses and dark skirts, beads and hats. Yet some wore the same clothes as the village workers.

Jack watched them from the fort and wondered. He had their blood. But he couldn't bring himself to visit them. He wasn't sure why. Maggie said her Ojibway family–his kin– had moved to the middle of the state and no longer made summer trips to Mackinac Island like the others. She hoped to visit them this fall. And she wanted Jack to go with her.

The thought of family led him to send another letter to his Uncle Patrick in Boston. Jack had written him that all was well and he would be there come summer's end. But he hadn't mentioned Maggie. He wasn't sure why. Maybe they did know about her. Maybe his grandparents had told Patrick, their first born, about their abandoned niece. Jack's blood raged less now when he thought of Maggie being left behind. It seemed to bother him more than it did her. Still, it wasn't right they had been raised apart. He wondered.

Could he go to Boston without her? Could he be the one to part them this time?

As he plunked his money onto the counter for writing papers, Jack wondered if he should give his uncle a specific week. The longer he stayed on this island, the harder it would be to leave. But if he told himself he could stay, he'd never find the truth about his father.

Jack knew he was becoming comfortable. Life was full with his musician duty, Maggie, his garden, and his new friends.

Walking out onto the street, Jack was overwhelmed by the vibrancy of life here; families, workers, bicycles, horses, well–dressed ladies carrying parasols that matched their dress, carriages lined up along the street awaiting fares, dandies and their ladies streaming across the street from Arnold Transit Docks, servants carrying luggage. Streets brimmed with tourists in their finery, female village workers in their long dark skirts, blouses and aprons, the men in dungarees, linen shirts and hats. Dogs yapped at bicycles and carriages topped with fine ladies and men on their way to the Island House or Mission House to the east of the fort.

Jack had promised himself that he would have the

label 'deserter' removed from his father's name in the fort records.

From time to time an older soldier would take him aside, throw his arm around Jack's shoulder and explain that men deserted the army for different reasons. That didn't mean they were all bad men. Some left for women, they'd say. Jack told himself that couldn't be the case with his father. Others left because they wanted to pursue other business opportunities. And some just didn't care for a soldier's life.

Jack couldn't understand any of it. He loved the order of this life; the brotherhood of the men. This magical island. He never tired of the blooming beauty of nature surrounding him. The blending blue of water and sky. The freshness of every breath. The squawk and mew of seagulls. The serenity of the lake.

Never had he had so many friends at one time. Back home in Ohio he'd had Fred Buckley as a best friend when they were younger, but Jack really spent most of his time on the farm working. A trip into Kendall Plains was half a day's journey by horse and usually they only traveled to town for supplies or a special event.

Mackinac Island suited Jack.

Jack didn't want to play.

Sergeant MacDougal had asked him to play his fiddle at

Friday night's Astor House hop as a 'favor' to him. He'd even wrangled Jack a twenty-four-hour leave to do so. The sergeant was proud of Jack's fiddling ability and felt sharing Jack's skills with the village would promote a good relationship between the village and Fort Mackinac.

Jack hated being the center of attention. He'd learned the only good thing about playing his fiddle at a dance was that he didn't have to dance. He also knew he'd never attend a dance unless it was to play his fiddle.

The night of the dance, Jack and Seth Anders arrived at the hotel shortly before the festivities were to begin.

The dance was held in a large room at Astor House. It reminded Jack of a barn loft at home where he'd fiddled at dances many a time.

A barn loft he was used to.

Here he was to stand on a small stage. He thought it too close to the dance floor.

Especially when Maggie arrived on Daniel's arm.

IO

"You look fine"

Jack almost didn't recognize his sister.

Maggie's straight dark hair had been scooped up and back leaving small tendrils to dance about her face. For the life of him, Jack couldn't figure out how all that thick hair could be held up like that without some kind of rope. The small pink hair ribbons she wore couldn't have been enough. Her dangling earrings made her look years older. And he couldn't imagine where she got her dress.

She floated in wearing a full-skirted pink dress with a bustle in back and a row of flat silk bows that traveled from her slim neck to the narrow circle of her waist. Her waist sash and dress hem shone of silk. A tiny pink purse dangled from the hand that wasn't draped over Daniel's arm as he escorted her into the room.

Daniel gave Jack a slight nod and a smirk as he steered Maggie to a table and pulled the chair out to seat her. Maggie's face lit and she waved when she saw Jack.

Jack yanked several fingernails from his teeth.

"Seth." Jack called to his friend.

Seth had been talking to a pretty brown-haired young lady with a blue bow in her hair seated in a row of chairs along the wall.

"She wrote my name on her dance card," he boasted to Jack, indicating the girl with the blue hair bow.

Jack's shoulders hunched in disgust.

"I thought you didn't like to dance." He almost sounded accusatory.

Seth shrugged. "Not with just anyone, but. . ."

"Listen, I need a favor."

Seth sighed and looked up at Jack who now stood a good head taller than him on the stage. Jack moved Seth around so he faced the room now crowding with well-dressed men and women. He centered Seth's sightline toward Maggie's table.

"See that girl in pink sitting with the stupid blond boy?"

"How do you know he's. . ."

"Trust me," said Jack. "I need you to keep an eye on him. Get on her dance card if you have to. I don't want her spending the entire evening with him."

Seth smiled. "She looks too pretty for you. I think I should. . . Oww!" He reeled from a light smack on the head.

"She's my sister!"

A puzzled expression washed over Seth then disappeared. He looked back at Maggie and Daniel.

"Fine. I'll do it." He faced Jack, walking backwards

through the crowd. "But only because you're my friend."

Jack started warming up his fiddle. He pulled his grandfather's handkerchief from a back pocket to use on his chin rest. A sheet listing the songs he would be playing that evening sat on a small round table behind him. He worked at sitting comfortably on the stool, although mostly he stood when he played. How could he sit?

Because magic embraced Jack when he fiddled. He moved and danced to the music as if he were another person. If he'd ever seen himself play, eyes closed, bow sliding across the strings with a furious passion, he would have claimed it wasn't him. Not quiet, shy Jack Murphy.

"You look so handsome in your uniform." Maggie oozed with maturity standing in front of her brother.

She looked even prettier up close. He scanned the now crowded room for Seth.

"You've seen me in it before." Adjusting a tuning peg, Jack added, "There are lots of soldiers here tonight."

She swayed, her full skirt swinging like a bell. "You haven't said anything about how I look tonight."

Jack checked his chin rest for comfort. "You look fine."

She gave him a sisterly stare of disgust as Daniel joined them in front of the stage. He held two glasses of punch.

"Here you are, Sweetheart." He handed Maggie a glass.

Jack liked this nickname even less than 'Maggie May'.

"Inga will be here, Jack," said Maggie. "Will you be able to talk with her when you take a break?"

"I don't get a break."

"You must get a break!"

Jack shrugged.

She changed the subject.

"Who's the soldier you came with?"

Jack noticed Daniel immediately glanced in the direction of Seth who conversed with an older man across the room.

"Corporal Seth Anders." Jack smiled at Daniel as he spoke. "You should dance with him tonight. He's a good friend of mine."

"Maybe I will," she said, swishing her skirts in a playful tease. "That is if Daniel will let me."

Almost over tightening his tuning peg, Jack slid his bow over the strings. A man dressed in a black suit and vest made his way over to the stage.

"Ladies and gentlemen," he announced as people shushed each other. "Welcome to the Astor House."

He introduced Jack as Musician Jack Murphy of Fort Mackinac and praised Captain Brady for allowing Jack to grace their presence this evening. Then Jack fiddled and couples danced and the room became a moving kaleidoscope of dark blue soldier uniforms, women's rainbow dresses, and the black and brown of men's cloth suits.

As he fiddled, Jack noted Seth talking to Maggie at her table. He smiled. Then he saw Maggie invite Inga to sit with them and introduce her to Seth. Jack stopped smiling.

Although, he thought, if Seth liked Inga then he wouldn't have to. And Maggie might leave him alone. The thought enticed him for a few seconds. At least for tonight, he decided, he needed Seth to watch Maggie.

Finishing his song, Jack ignored the applause and called Seth over.

"You're supposed to be spending time with my sister. Not Inga."

"But your sister's taken and Inga's cute."

Jack looked over at the table. "Her nose is too small."

Seth followed his gaze. "No it's not. She's cute."

Scanning the room as he prepared for his next song, Jack asked, "Where's Daniel?" Part of him hoped the bounder had abandoned his sister. That would certainly make things easier. Then he would definitely give Seth permission to spend time with Inga.

"I think he went out back with some friends," Seth said.

Unfortunately for Jack, Daniel soon rejoined Maggie. Jack's teeth ground as he watched them dance. He didn't like Daniel's hand around her waist. Or the way he held her hand. Or the way she laughed and looked like she was enjoying herself.

Although he did have a few short breaks throughout the evening, Jack didn't speak with Inga. He just sat on his stool and sipped a glass of punch.

Safe from blond girls with too small noses.

As the evening progressed, Jack's fiddling became livelier. He played more polkas, reels and jigs. Dancers whirled each other across the dance floor faster and faster, laughing wildly when the song ended.

Jack had been so caught up in playing his music that he hadn't noticed Maggie's absence. Tradition held that the last song of the evening would be slow so, after mopping his brow with his grandfather's handkerchief, Jack played "The Gentle Maiden." A waltz, it had been one of his grandma's favorites.

Couple by couple, the crowd started to disperse. Jack wiped his fiddle and placed it in its case. He couldn't locate Maggie in the thinning crowd. Seth jumped up on the edge of the stage.

"Have you seen my sister?" Jack asked.

"Not for awhile," he said. "But I did dance with her twice." His eyes smiled. "She's not only lovely, she's quite charming."

Hopping off the stage, they left Astor House. Market Street teamed with couples leaving the dance. While waiting for several carriages to pass by, Jack heard a commotion from the alley behind Astor House. The alley noise blended with the loud conversations, laughter and carriage rumblings of the street.

But for some reason Jack felt a need to explore it.

He tugged at Seth's uniform sleeve and pulled him through people in the direction of the noise. As they drew closer, a female plea became distinct.

"Daniel! You're not yourself. Take me home, please!"

A loud slap and a weak cry filled the air.

Maggie.

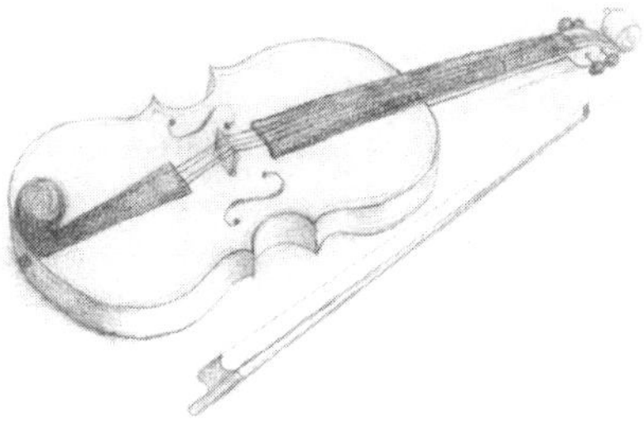

— 11 —

"Smelly old coot"

Jack and Seth raced down the side of Astor House, turning the corner into the back alley. Without slowing down, Jack jumped on Daniel's back.

"What the. . .get off me!" Daniel yelled, twirling in circles, trying to shake Jack loose.

Maggie leaned against the back of the building, hand covering her cheek, tears streaming. As Seth went to see if she was all right, Daniel shook Jack free and attacked Seth from behind.

"Arrrgghhh!" Daniel yelled, plowing full force into Seth's back, slamming him into the building.

"Stop it!" Maggie screamed.

Seth tried to hold Daniel's arms from behind but he couldn't contain Daniel's mouth.

"You're just a girl! You can't tell me what to do...you're nothing but a half-breed!"

Jack punched Daniel in the face.

"He's been drinking," cried Maggie. "He doesn't know what he's doing."

"Maybe he doesn't," Jack huffed for breath, trying to shake the pain from his punching hand, "but I do."

"I'm bleeding!" Daniel's high pitched scream shocked the night.

A tiny blood rivulet trickled from his nose.

Grabbing Daniel by the collar, Jack confronted him. "Don't you ever come near my sister again."

When Jack released his collar, Daniel disappeared like a thief into the night. Still laboring for breath, Jack turned and watched Seth gently place his uniform jacket over Maggie's hunched shoulders. Jack didn't know what to say to her.

When she folded sobbing into his arms, he knew he didn't have to say anything.

"Thank you for the use of your jacket, Corporal Anders." Maggie removed the warm wool from her shoulders and handed it to Seth.

"You're welcome, Miss Murphy."

The three of them stood at the bottom of the staircase leading to Maggie's room. Jack had promised to stay there tonight and help her pack and move in with Ellie the next day.

"You won't get into any trouble. . .with your

commanding officers for fighting, I hope," said Maggie.

"No," said Seth. "No legal authorities were involved so . . . I'll be fine."

"I won't get into any trouble either," Jack offered from the bottom step.

The streetlamp illuminated Seth's face.

"Oh, you're hurt!" Maggie cooed. He smiled as she reached his puffing eyebrow. "You should put some ice on that," she said.

Jack's left hand throbbed. "My hand's fine, thank you."

He watched a few seconds before interrupting.

"I'll be back at the fort tomorrow," Jack said, pulling Maggie away. "Thanks for helping. You can go now." He pushed Seth toward the fort.

Laughing, Seth bid them both good night, his voice lingering on "Miss Murphy."

"You may call me Maggie if you like," she offered.

His footsteps echoed down the empty street. Walking backwards, he faced them. "I'd be honored. Maggie."

Jack turned Maggie around and followed her up the stairs.

"Corporal Anders is such a gentleman," she gushed.

Imagining the evening could have turned out much worse, Jack smiled. "He's a saint. I'll sit out here while you get ready for bed."

Maggie disappeared behind the door. Jack removed his fiddle from his back to sit on the steps. He checked it to make sure it hadn't been damaged in the tussle.

Sticking her head out the door, Maggie said, "I'm sorry

about your hand," before disappearing again.

Fisting and opening his left hand, Jack grimaced with pain. Then smiled.

"I'm not."

"Hang on, Murphy!"

A scratchy laugh accompanied Private Bogart's command from the neighboring rowboat. Corporal Karls sat in the seat behind Jack, jostling and jiggling.

Not a problem, Jack told himself over and over, trying to ignore his buddies' helpful jeers. He pulled the oars with all his might. *I can do this.*

Jack concentrated on Round Island coming closer within his sights. The bigger it seemed, the closer he was. He tried to gauge how many rows he had left until they touched sand. Maybe fifty. Fifty-five?

"Almost there, Jack," Seth comforted from Bogart's boat.

When they had received permission to take the fort boats to Round Island on the beautiful June afternoon, Jack had offered to row. He thought if he had something to focus on other than the deep hungry water beneath him, he could make the trip. And he wouldn't be alone in case anything happened. At least that's how Seth had convinced him to come. Besides, thought Jack, maybe he wouldn't live on an island forever, but he was determined to conquer this fear.

In some strange way, proving he wasn't a coward proved the same about his father. If he wasn't a coward, neither was his father.

It was all he had right now.

Pulling the boats onto shore, Jack worked hard to appear nonchalant even as he breathed normally for the first time since leaving Mackinac Island. Backing onto the beach with a stronghold on the boat, Jack peered across the harbor at the Island. It was the first time he'd seen it from afar since coming here on the passenger ship in April. It seemed impossible that he'd only been on this island a matter of weeks.

It had been snowing, he remembered, wiping stinging sweat out of his eyes. He supposed Mackinac Island could resemble a turtle, as Indian lore maintained. But he didn't really see it as that. Somehow, in the few weeks since he'd arrived, Mackinac Island had become like...

"Pull away, Murph," Corporal Karls interrupted Jack's thoughts. "We ended up with a heavier load than those ne're do wells." The corporal nodded at Private Bogart and Seth whose rowboat sat several feet up the beach.

Sighing, Jack pulled hard on the bow. As he shaded his eyes from the early afternoon sun to see across the smooth glittering harbor waters, a sense of pride tingled through him. He'd rowed the entire way and survived.

In return for a fat wicker basket lunch, they'd promised Dutch a slew of whitefish, perch and lake trout.

A uniform jacket landed on Jack's head. Shirts and fatigue caps followed.

“Hey, Murph,” yelled Private Jaspers from the beach where he sat unlacing his boots. “Why don’t you take care of Dutch’s basket here while we cool off?”

Jack smiled. It didn’t bother him now that his friends teased him about his fear of water. He’d rowed across. He’d made it.

“Happy to,” Jack returned. “I may even leave you a crumb or two.”

Jaspers and the others dove into the waves.

While they splashed and cavorted in the cool blue waters, Jack set the lunch basket in the shade of the forest trees several yards from the beach. He left the fishing gear in the boats.

Removing his socks and boots, Jack rolled up his pant cuffs. Better.

The air felt scared rabbit still. No sign of movement. He couldn’t recall a June day this hot in Ohio.

Watching his friends, imagining the water spreading cool through their bodies, Jack stood and walked to the lake’s edge.

Maybe just to cool off, he thought.

As long as it doesn’t go over my knees.

Rock strewn Mackinac Island beaches left marks on his feet. Here muddy sand oozed between his toes; soothing, cooling, and amusing.

Seth swam close to the shore and Jack, Jack’s hatless hair a vibrant red in the sun, water lapping about his calves.

“You ever try swimming?” Seth asked.

Jack shook his head.

"Nope." He smiled into the dazzling blue water and a bobbing Seth several feet out from him. Jack enjoyed the rhythmic rush of water to and from his legs. This was enough for him. "And I'm not planning on it any time soon."

"You do live on an island, you know."

Seth heard nothing but seagulls, water washing onto shore and their friends' laughter.

"I taught my little sister to swim when she was five," Seth said, treading closer to shore.

Jack's head whipped back with laughter.

"That makes me feel better. A girl. All of five, eh?" He watched his feet muck about in the shallow water. "Thanks."

Jack smiled.

"If you tell me your intentions toward my sister."

"Why?"

"I know you," Jack said, swirling spirals in the hip deep water with his hands. "Once you get your mind set, you're mule stubborn. So...if you want to teach me to swim," his smile and spirals broadened, "tell me your intentions toward Maggie."

Seth looked around, noting the others at a distance.

"This isn't really the time and place I..."

"It's a fine time and place," interrupted Jack. His smile reflected the sun.

"Are you gonna let me teach you to swim?"

"Are you gonna tell me your intentions toward Maggie?"

Seth offered his hands. Jack stepped closer, the water

threatening his waist now.

"You first," Jack insisted.

"But..."

"Who knows how long it will take me to learn this swimming thing. Just tell me straight out and get it over with."

Sighing, Seth shook his head.

"You'd better be a fast learner."

"I'm waiting." Jack's hands now swirled counterclockwise spirals in the water at his waist.

"Fine." Seth squinted from the sun, glanced at the beach, then gazed directly into Jack's steely eyes. "She means a great deal to me. And I promise to treat her with respect and... not lie to her..."

"And...?"

"Well, Hell's Bells, Jack, I don't know much else!"

Nodding, Jack smiled. "That's enough for now."

"Now your turn. Take your hands and ..."

"I could eat a horse, two cows and all their kin!" declared Private Jaspers.

Lightening fast, Jack retracted his arms just before a huge splash deluged him. Sputtering, he noted Seth's smile and a mouthed, *you owe me*, as the two joined their friends on shore in time to argue over the contents of Dutch's picnic basket.

As long as he could row a boat, he wouldn't need to worry about swimming, Jack told himself before slapping Private Bogart's hand away from the strawberry jam.

~ ~ ~

After sounding Recall from Fatigue, Jack and Fool walked over to the Commissary on an errand for Dutch. He needed more potatoes. For a change. Jack was tempted to stop by the hospital to see Maggie. He could see the building from the Commissary. He'd seen her there earlier dressed in her long gray skirt, high collared white blouse and white apron. She looked prim.

But prim was good. Because Seth saw her daily now that she worked at the fort.

Mostly Jack was pleased Maggie and Seth liked each other. He'd stated on Round Island that his intentions were acceptable. And he was certainly a better match for Maggie than Daniel. Jack had even asked Seth if he'd heard the slurs Daniel had cast at Maggie. What he had called her the night of the dance.

A half breed.

Jack liked most of the soldiers in the barracks and got along with all of them. He just ignored the fights they had amongst themselves, usually over money or women. But he'd also heard some of them talk. About Metis. About never marrying a woman with Indian blood.

Seth said he'd heard the slur targeting Maggie but thought nothing of it. Metis was just another people to him, he'd said. Some people were Irish, some German, some French, some Indian and so forth. He'd shrugged. And some were a little bit of each. That explanation had suited Jack fine. Made sense to him, he realized. Maybe he wasn't so unusual.

Several cool rainy days finally passed and the sun warmed the island again. With the arrival of June, baseball had become keen on everyone's minds. Practices were held afternoons and evenings as possible. A few games had been played against a village team and a few more were scheduled with teams from Reed City and St. Ignace.

The thought of baseball made Jack smile as he approached the Commissary. He called Fool away from investigating a bug in the dirt. Jack was thinking about the sprouting green in his garden this morning, his boot just stepping onto the wooden Commissary porch, when a foul smell smacked him in the face. Made his nose twitch.

A smell of garlic and onion and. . .someone who hadn't changed clothes for a year or so.

Entering the Commissary, Jack saw the origin of the odor.

Sitting on the bench under the window was a small, crusty old man with a perky-eared black dog. Jack was sure they shared fleas, could almost see them springing from one to the other. The old man wore tattered pants, a filthy buckskin jacket and moccasins that reached mid-leg with top stitching along the foot that made the toe curl around the edges. A colorful beaded belt encircled his midsection while another smaller belt decorated his battered wide brimmed leather hat. Gray and white whiskers sprouted with random unevenness from the million crags in his face like weeds from beneath rocks. His thick mustache twirled into a fine stiff point at either end.

Jack thought he saw a dried brown food substance in it.

A single gray inch-wide braid dangled to his waist while the rest of his hair clumped at his thin shoulders in greasy gray sections. A rifle rested across his lap.

The man swashed his mouth with his tongue before spewing a brown stream into the brass spittoon next to Mac's desk. His beady eyes about crinkled closed when he smiled, a smile that boasted an empty front space between coffee brown teeth. He whistled through his nose when he breathed. A round box the size of a large boulder was set next to him on the bench.

The old man's eyes slithered to Jack. He offered a leather pouch.

"Chaw?" the man asked, his voice higher and huskier than Jack might have thought.

Jack just shook his head and looked for another place to sit and wait for Mac. The bench beckoned. Fool finally found his way in and the two dogs growled, hair raised, ears back.

"Non, Aloin." With the man's soft words, the black dog stopped growling and sat.

"Go lay down," Jack commanded Fool who slowly made his way to the other side of the room where Jack had pointed.

Jack stood in the doorway to the storeroom. "Hey Mac," he yelled. "Dutch sent me for potatoes."

Mac called back for him to have a seat and he would be with him in a minute.

That wasn't what Jack wanted to hear.

Sitting at the end of the bench, Jack stared out the

window.

"You got you chien dere, little man."

Figuring the man must be talking to him as he was the only person in the room, Jack looked at him. The man gestured to Fool across the room.

"He's my dog," said Jack.

"Dogs." The man spoke through the wad of tobacco in his cheek. "Dey loyal forever, eh?"

Jack nodded. He had never heard the melodic way this man talked. The up and down of it. It differed from Dutch or Mac's manner of speech.

"What name you dog, little man?"

Jack frowned and wasn't going to answer him. "Fool."

Slapping one hand on his knee, the man yelled, "Ooohhweeeeee, dat good name for pup!" He settled back, scratching his dog behind the ears.

"You name you chien?" he asked.

"No," said Jack.

The man stared at him. A minute passed. Another.

"My grandpa named him," Jack finally offered, searching the doorway for Mac's shadow. "When he was a pup."

"You grand pa, eh?" The man pronounced the word 'grandpa' carefully and smiled. "This my chien. Aloin." Hearing his name, the black dog panted at the old man. "It mean noble friend. Chien—dogs—dey likes family, eh? Never do you wrong. Loyal," he said. "Loyal chien."

Just as Jack was wondering if the old man knew he was repeating himself, Mac appeared in the doorway carrying a lumpy burlap sack. To Jack's surprise, he greeted the small smelly man with a warm smile.

"JB. You're here early this year." Mac slapped the man on the shoulder and they shook hands.

"I want you to greet . . .before I work. Good to see you, Mon ami," said the old man.

He gathered his box and dog, the knives and hunting tools attached to his belt clanking like a tinker's pots and pans, nodded at Jack, and left.

"Here are your potatoes, Lad."

Tossing the bag over his shoulder, Jack thanked Mac and jerked his thumb at the door. "What's that smelly old coot doing here?"

Mac stopped. He looked Jack in the eye. "Watch your mouth, Lad," he warned sharply. "That's your grandfather you're talking about."

— 12 —

"Sealing a vow"

Jack's jaw fell. He had to concentrate in order to hold the bag on his shoulder.

"What do you mean?"

"Your sister didn't tell you?" asked Mac.

Jack could only shake his head.

"Jack, that 'old coot' is your mother's father. J. B. Roy," explained Mac. "Trapping not what it used to be, he comes here every summer to work at the Island House for Mrs. Van Allen. Cleaning, gardening and such."

The bag of potatoes now felt like a bag of bricks.

"Why does. . .he talks funny."

Mac chuckled. "He's French-Canadian, Lad. They have their own way of mixing English and French, but the more you listen to him the easier he is to understand. You had trouble understanding my Scot way of talking at first now, didn't you?" he added.

Jack couldn't think of what to say so he turned to leave.

“JB can make music come out of that squeezebox of his like nobody you ever heard,” Mac said. He smiled. “Must be where you get your musical talent.”

Mac couldn’t see the horror that crossed Jack’s face with his words.

“He spent some time with your pa,” Mac offered. He hesitated, making sure Jack had heard him before returning to the storeroom.

Standing in the middle of the Commissary office alone, a peculiar sensation punched Jack in his gut: like he didn’t know where he came from or where he was headed.

Like he was caught between day and night, unable to enter either.

Caught in a twilight at this fort. On this island.

Through the barracks hallway to the kitchen, Jack thought about how that old man stank and spit. His filthy clothes. Mac had said Jack got his musical ability from that old coot. Jack decided it wasn’t so.

That nasty, filthy, funny-talking old man couldn’t be his grandfather.

The light-headed twilight feeling shifted into a feisty fiery one that spread through his belly and into his jaw.

His grandfather was a big strapping Irish man with short white hair, a ruddy clean face, who had worked the land all his life and was buried under an oak tree next to his grandmother. That straggly haired little man who had sat across from him was not his grandfather. No kin of his.

Jack tossed the bag of potatoes on the kitchen table.

“What’s with you, Murph?” asked Private Stanton as he

peeled the last of the potatoes in front of him. "Thanks for the potatoes. Just what I wanted."

No smart reply came from Jack like it usually did. He just looked at the private and stuttered, "You're. . . you're welcome." And left.

After sounding Recall from Drill at one o'clock, he went to find Maggie.

Unable to locate his sister on the first floor, Jack had clambered up the stairs to the second floor of the hospital.

Soldiers occupied three of the ten beds in the ward. Short white cotton curtains stirred in the sultry afternoon breeze. A butterfly alighted on the back of a chair, fluttered its bright beauty and floated out an open window.

"Why didn't you tell me?"

"SSShhhhhh." Maggie placed her forefinger to her lips.

Setting her tray of neatly aligned surgical instruments on a table, she faced her brother. "What are you talking about? Why don't you wait until I'm done here?"

"Do you get a break or something?" he asked.

"I can probably leave for a few minutes," she said, folding a white cloth over the surgical tray. "Let me check with the steward first."

When she returned, her starched white apron and cap had been removed and she wore only her gray skirt and white blouse. Her wealth of shiny hair was neatly coiled into a bun.

"I have ten minutes."

Leaving the white railed porch, they strolled along the side of the hospital. Maggie wanted to walk in the shade.

"It's unusually warm for this time of year on the island," she said, smoothing her skirts as she walked. "Now what's so important you need to speak with me right now?"

"Why didn't you tell me about this. . .JB. . .person?"

"So JB's here?" Maggie smiled. "He's a bit early this year."

"Sergeant MacDougal said he knew our father."

"I suppose he did," she said. " I don't recall."

"Why do you call him JB if he's your grandfather?"

Jack couldn't imagine calling his grandfather anything but grandpa.

Maggie shrugged. "I don't know. Everyone calls him JB."

Jack didn't know how to say it so he just blurted it. "How can a filthy old coot like that. . .be our. . .be related?"

Maggie stopped mid–stride. Her look reminded him, for a flash, of his grandmother's look when Jack had forgotten to do a chore.

"Jack, he's our grandfather. And he's more than what you see. I'm sorry I didn't tell you about him, but I don't think you. . ."

"He's no kin of mine." Shaking his head, Jack spoke from his heart. "And he's for sure not my grandfather!"

She pointed toward a bench under the umbrella of a maple. "Jack," she said softly as she sat, "he's family."

Jack lost control of his voice as it squeaked and wavered. "Maggie." He grabbed her hands. "If you could only have known our grandfather. . .Papa's father. He was. . . big and smart and. . . he was. . . how could a man like JB be our grandfather?"

Maggie withdrew her hands. "He wasn't really around much. Our grandmother—JB's wife— was Ojibway. She died shortly after Mama was born. Mama was raised by her mother's people."

Jack was afraid to ask. "He. . . JB. . . left?"

"Yes, Jack, he left." Maggie's manner was matter of fact. "That's what trappers do. They leave for months at a time to trap beaver and fox. He knew his daughter was well cared for with family."

Jack leaned against the tree, his face and hair dappled by sun and shade. When he didn't speak or look her way for several minutes, she rose, smoothed her skirts, and walked back to the hospital.

Jack was glad when heavy gray clouds rolled in that evening forcing the cancellation of baseball practice. Although he figured he was mad enough to smack a baseball to Round Island. Might feel good, he thought.

Sitting on the barracks' front porch he watched the rain. And he thought. He pondered more than a body should ever have to.

Puckering his lips, he practiced "I'll Take You Home Again, Kathleen." He had promised Mac he would play it for the Sunday dress parade. Mac said if he had to listen to Private Hockley butcher his favorite song one more time the good private was likely to wake one morning to find his bugle straightened.

Why hadn't Maggie told him about JB if she knew he was coming here? If he came every year?

When had he last seen their father, Jack wondered.

Jack stopped playing. He knew for dang sure he hadn't inherited *anything* from that filthy old coot. Especially not his music.

He started playing the song again. He wanted to please Mac. Unshed tears welled tight and hot, his head feeling like a roasted potato about to explode. But he kept playing. He hadn't cried since his grandmother's death and he wasn't about to start now.

Not over a stupid old coot like JB.

Never will I call him my grandfather Jack thought.

And spit into the rain to seal his vow.

13

"Tarnation"

Talk in the barracks was of the upcoming baseball game at the fort against Reed City. But opinions became stronger and louder when discussion turned to the highly touted Fourth of July game against the Diamond Base Ball Club in Cheboygan.

"Ain't no way we're gonna lose that game on the Fourth," declared Private Hiram Eddy, the Never Sweats' pitcher. His blacksmith's arms bulged beneath his uniform.

Lieutenant Pratt's copy of *Spaulding's Base Ball Guide* was floating around the barracks with the promise that it would be returned to him the next day. Talk among the men had to do with the starting line up, injuries, and the twenty-five dollar prize for the winner. Lieutenant Pratt decided the Never Sweats needed a practice game. He had contacted men from the village team and challenged them to a game.

Besides baseball, the talk was of the Fourth festivities in the village. Private Johnsen boasted of having won the pie eating contest for the last three years running. Just looking at him, Jack could see he was a man dedicated to his sport. The men often even sacrificed their dessert so he could practice. Due to side effects of his pie eating talent, the private didn't have to worry about playing at the Never Sweats game and missing all the Fourth of July festivities. When Private Muldune asked if Johnsen was thinking of entering the tight rope walking contest, a united belly laugh erupted among the men.

Jack lay on his cot reading a new book called *The Adventures of Huckleberry Finn.* He hadn't spoken to Maggie since that afternoon at the Post Hospital a few days ago. He hadn't seen JB either. Jack figured the old coot must be too busy working at the Island House to bother him. That suited Jack just fine

But when he and Corporal Noggins were asked to run over to the Island House to pick up a barrel of flour that had mistakenly been delivered there instead of the fort, Jack didn't try to get out of it.

He probably could have. Mac might have sent someone else if Jack had pleaded Dutch needed him or he needed to practice his music. That got him to wondering why Mac had asked him to go to the Island House in the first place. Knowing the old coot worked there and all.

Jack had walked and ridden by the Island House a few times delivering supplies, but he'd never visited the popular summer resort.

"He's all hitched and ready to go, Murph," offered Corporal Noggins, checking the fit of Lulu May's huge dapple grey rear to the wagon harness.

"Lulu May is a she, not a he." Jack wondered why he had to state the obvious. But the more he worked with the corporal whose mouth hung open with a permanent invitation to flies, the more evident it became that obvious was necessary.

"Right," the corporal agreed, smiling. His straggly goatee looked like it actually belonged on a goat, not a twenty-something corporal from Alabama whose words twanged like a jaw harp.

They had to wait to let a shiny black rig filled with finely dressed people leave from in front of the Island House before Lulu May could pull the wagon up the deeply rutted side drive to the back. The kitchen delivery entrance boasted stacked barrels and crates, but no people.

"Y'all got flour for the fort?" Corporal Noggins screeched from his perch on the wagon seat.

Jack shook his head in an attempt to eliminate the corporal's twangy scream and jumped off the wagon seat.

"I'll find someone," Jack said. "You stay here." Jack pointed decidedly at the corporal. "Stay."

If Fool could do it, thought Jack, maybe the corporal could too. Maybe.

Kitchen heat added to the heat of the June day. Jack figured since it was just after lunch time, many of the kitchen workers might be on break. But when he entered the kitchen proper, several cooks chopped and stirred at their various stations.

Jack felt a sudden rush of relief. No JB.

"Help ya, soldier?" an older cook asked as he wiped his hands on a cloth.

"Yes, Sir," said Jack. "Looking for a barrel of flour delivered here instead of the fort?"

"Yup," said the cook. "I just got to get the bill for you to sign. Be right back. You hungry?" he asked, indicating a pot on a stove. "Got some stew left over from lunch."

"No, thank you, Sir," said Jack, hoping the man didn't hear his rumbling stomach. He didn't want to stay any longer than need be. Just in case.

Flour barrel loaded onto the wagon, Jack and Corporal Noggins were half way down the drive when the corporal stopped Lulu May.

"Would you looky that!" he exclaimed. "Ain't never seen such flowers and finery at a house. It's like a weddin's goin' on all the time!"

Jack shared his view of the Island House; roses climbed trellises to the porch, their fragrance drifting in the heat of the summer afternoon, while smaller colorful flowers bordered the dirt walkway. Mostly greenery, neatly trimmed, covered the lawn area in front.

"It looked the same when we got here. It's great. Let's go," Jack ordered. It didn't matter that he was a private and Noggins was a corporal. Jack wanted to leave before...

JB. There he stood. Watering the flowers below the front porch with a huge bucket. A lady dressed in a striped bronze-colored skirt with a bustle, wearing a full-sleeved blouse with high puffy hair walked out of the Island House onto the wide white railed porch. Jack could hear the rustle of her silky skirts amidst the seagull calls in the afternoon calm. She hailed JB.

"Get up, Lulu May." Jack had grabbed the reins from the corporal.

But Lulu May had found a few blades of sweet grass to enjoy beside the drive.

"Oui, Madame Van Allen," JB croaked as she approached him, removing his hat in deference.

"JB, you've done it again." Mrs. Van Allen smiled, gesturing to the lawn and flowers. "I don't know what I'd do without you."

Hat held in front of his chest, JB bowed slightly as he thanked her again. Jack didn't want to speak, to draw attention to the wagon. So he tried swatting the reins across Lulu May's mammoth butt as quietly as possible.

"I'll need the porch furniture painted, of course. Just one chair at a time so as not to inconvenience any of our guests." She addressed JB with a smile. "Do fetch a lemonade from the kitchen when you get thirsty."

"Oui, Madame Van Allen." JB bowed. "Merci, Madame."

She turned to leave, Jack finally getting Lulu May's rear to move forward, when Corporal Noggins waved at the porch.

"Hey JB!" he called just as Jack guided the wagon into the street.

Out of his right eye, Jack caught JB's hand raised in greeting from the porch.

"Hey, that was JB!" the corporal stated, as thrilled as if

he'd been given a twenty-four-hour pass. "You know he plays that squeezebox purdier than..."

"I know." Jack interrupted, his eyes focused on the street and Lulu May's rear. "I know."

When Seth approached Jack on his cot, Jack thought maybe he wanted to make plans for their next time off. Although Seth had been spending much of his time off as of late with Maggie. But Seth had informed Jack that Captain Brady wanted to see him.

At first Jack wondered if maybe Captain Brady had discovered something about his father. But the captain was 'requesting' Jack play in the fort military band for the Fourth of July. Jack saluted and promised to attend the remaining scheduled band practices.

And knew for sure he wouldn't be fulfilling his substitute player role in the big Fourth of July baseball game.

Stopping at the lower gun platform before heading back to the barracks, Jack viewed the village below.

It thrived even as daylight faded. Tired babies cried, their nannies soothing.

Carriages conveyed people from their hotels to dinner and from dinner to hotels. A man's voice carried to the fort as he sang "My Darling Clementine" loudly and off-key. A curtain of lavender and yellow the shade of crocus sprouting from behind the fort kitchen brightened the edge of sky where it melted into the lake. Fading lilacs scented the air.

Jack wondered if Boston ever looked, sounded or smelled anything like this island.

The next evening after returning from band practice, Jack hoped to read for awhile. His book was getting good. Private Hockley had taken evening duty so Jack could attend practice.

That worked for Jack. He needed to get to his garden as early as possible tomorrow. He might even have to cut his morning kitchen time with Dutch short. There was so much work to do and with the holiday coming, it would likely be ignored for a few days. The garden was as green and thick as Jack could have hoped. He was sure of a good crop. Regret tinged his thoughts: wouldn't his grandpa be proud of him.

His real grandpa. Grandpa Murphy. It irritated Jack that he made that distinction to himself. He wondered about what Mac had said.

About the old coot knowing his father. Maybe he would ask him someday.

Maybe not.

Jack had just washed up and was planning to lie on his cot and read himself to sleep early, when a knock rapped at the barracks' open door wall.

"Is there someone here called 'little man'?"

Privates Sims and Bookerton stopped playing checkers long enough to laugh and point at Jack.

"Littlest man we got is right there," said Private Sims.

Jack's stomach contracted. JB had called him little man.

"Nobody here answers to that name," Jack said, louder than he'd intended. He turned a page.

"Who's askin'?" Private Bookerton asked before jumping three of Private Sims' black checkers with his red one.

"Some old drunk. . . JD or somethin'. . . down at the Empire Saloon." The man spit off the barracks' porch. "Says his grandson is stationed here at the fort. Wants him to come fetch him so he don't get tossed in jail and fined money. I'm supposed to come back with a 'little man' from the fort's all I know," the man finished, pulling at his mustache.

"JB?" Private Sminton stopped polishing his boots and glanced at Jack. "He your grandpappy, Boy?"

Jack turned a page.

"I got a nickel in my pocket either way," said the man. Hiking the frayed suspenders that barely held up his pants, he spit and left.

That's that, Jack thought.

Soldiers resumed playing checkers, polishing boots and playing cards. Private Sminton played "Oh Dem Golden Slippers" on his harmonica. For the next ten minutes their collective sidelong glances chipped away at Jack.

"Tarnation!" he finally yelled, throwing his book on the floor, grabbing his jacket. "I'm going!"

~ ~ ~

A noise—a movement— caught his attention.

Corporal Seth Anders scanned the fort below from his South Sally Port sentry post.

Nothing moved now. Probably a squirrel or dog, he told himself. The village had quieted in the half hour since dark had claimed the island.

A bugle sounded Taps. The corporal figured it must be Private Hockley.

Although he smiled and decided Hockley's playing had improved.

A staggered movement joined a muffled groan and clinking from below.

"Password, soldier?" Seth demanded.

Silence.

The corporal removed his rifle from his shoulder. "Who goes there?"

"I forgot the dang password," a loud whisper floated through the dark.

Seth lowered his rifle.

"Jack?" he whispered. "That you?"

Several seconds passed. "Yeah."

"You don't recall today's password?"

"If I did remember the. . . blame password don't you think. . . I'd have said it by now?"

Seth labored to see Jack's outline in the faint glow of the village streetlamps below. "You drunk, Jack?" he asked with bewilderment.

Jack cut his own laugh short. "I wouldn't be dragging this. . . drunk old. . . coot up a hill if I were!" He grunted with effort as JB's hand flopped in his face for the third time. "Dang belt makes enough noise to wake the dead."

"What're you going to do with him?"

"Well," Jack maneuvered to avoid JB's breath on his face. "Didn't think that far."

"All's well," Seth called from his parapet. He had fifteen minutes before he had to repeat the call.

Jack felt himself pulled backward, felt JB's weight behind him and suddenly Jack was looking at the fort from the ground. But JB was standing now, all by himself. No, Jack realized, Seth had taken off JB's belt, hauled him upright and was almost trotting up the steps with him. Jumping up, Jack picked up the belt and clambered up the steps to reach them. Together they mostly carried JB through the fort entrance and up the few steps into the empty guardhouse. They tossed him onto the cot in the back cell.

"He can sleep it off here," said Seth.

Half bent over to catch his breath, Jack sputtered, "Thank. . . you, but. . . "

Shouldering the rifle he had momentarily leaned against the wall, Seth faced Jack. "I have to get back or. . . "

Jack's expression stopped Seth cold. He closed his eyes briefly before turning and opening them. First Sergeant Connors loomed like a fairy tale ogre in the guardhouse doorway. Both soldiers saluted him. Jack swallowed hard.

"Gone for a midnight stroll, have we, Corporal Anders?"

Jack tried to explain to the sergeant that Seth leaving his

sentry post was his fault. But the sergeant wouldn't hear any of it.

"You're relieved of duty, Corporal Anders, and you are remanded to your quarters until Assembly when I expect to see you standing in front of me in my office."

"Yes, Sir." Seth saluted again, waited for the sergeant to step back from the doorway.

Jack watched his friend march smartly across the parade ground to the dark barracks.

The first sergeant glanced into the cell room where JB snored on a cot, and back to Jack. "That JB with you?"

Jack sighed, bit his lip and closed his eyes before speaking. This was it. He would be kicked out of the army. He'd have to contact his aunt and uncle. Boston might be nice. "Yes, Sir."

"He your grandpa, boy?"

"No, sir," lied Jack.

Figuring he was already probably condemned to hell from lying about his age and enlisting when he planned to leave soon, Jack couldn't see one small lie making matters any worse. Once confessed, he would be saying Hail Marys and Our Fathers until snow flew.

And it was June.

The first sergeant's eyebrows raised and his head tilted with surprise. "Thought he was."

Approaching the cell, Sergeant Connors took a long look at JB snoring in the dark. He sniggered, withdrew a small pouch from his pocket, and stuffed a pinch of tobacco into his cheeks.

"Mind he leaves before Reveille, Boy." He stuffed the pouch back into his pocket.

Jack nodded.

"And," added First Sergeant Connors, "mind you stay in barracks until mornin' or the corporal there won't be the only one with a court martial on his record."

"Yes, Sir." Jack saluted, pivoted and left.

'Court Martial' rang in Jack's ears as he walked to barracks, stripped down and climbed into his cot. Court Martial. Jack wondered if Seth knew. Or, Jack thought with immediate relief, maybe the sergeant was just trying to scare Jack. His entire body relaxed. That was it. It was just a scare tactic like his grandpa had done so often. Jack smiled. Well, it worked, he thought.

Jack thought of sneaking into the kitchen to fetch Fool back to his cot before deciding he'd gotten into enough trouble for one night.

— 14 —

"A day to remember"

Before the crickets had even thought about chirping the next morning, Jack had checked the guardhouse. JB was gone, clanging belt and all. Jack didn't ask the sentry if he'd seen JB, but Corporal Riley had just smiled when Jack stopped by so early. He seemed relieved it wasn't an officer who had caught him 'resting.' Jack didn't ask about JB, and the corporal didn't offer information.

Corporal Seth Anders was to go before a garrison court martial immedately after the Fourth of July holiday. Jack couldn't believe it. Seth had only tried to help him. Help he wouldn't have needed if his. . . the old coot hadn't become drunk as a skunk and called for Jack.

So now, Jack thought, biting two nails at once, instead of JB sitting in a village jail for a night, Seth was facing court martial for 'dereliction of duty.'

When Jack discovered the officer serving as judge advocate for the court martial was Lieutenant Pratt, he held out hope for a light sentence. Seth would serve jail time until his trial, missing all the Fourth of July festivities. Jack sighed. Maggie wouldn't be happy about that. His sister had plans.

Punishment for Jack was a week of afternoon kitchen fatigue duty. He didn't think that was fair. He should have received the harsher punishment since it was his fault Seth had left his station. He would have switched places if he could. But all he could do was tell Seth he was sorry.

It was a mystery to Jack as to why everyone liked JB. Stuck in Jack's craw. Most of the soldiers seemed to enjoy listening to his trapping and hunting stories told in his strange backward French and English. They greeted him with a slap on the back and a smile. Jack had even spotted JB sitting with Mac in front of the Officers' Quarters, smoking that long pipe of his. Spitting and laughing. Aloin by his side.

Jack couldn't stand the sight of JB. Especially now. Maggie had told him that JB donated most of the coins he earned from playing music in the village to Ste. Anne's church. That JB attended Mass several times a week and lit candles for his departed loved ones. Jack had taken to saying a prayer as soon as he walked through the door of Ste. Anne's with Maggie on Sundays that he wouldn't run into JB there. So far his prayers had been answered.

Jack figured the old coot was just trying to buy his way to salvation. He sighed. And wondered how many more Hail Marys he would be assigned as penance after his next confession.

He knew JB stole from the Island House chef's herb garden. That he brought the ill-gotten gains to Dutch, who accepted them without asking where JB had 'found' them. Dutch was sweet on one of the officers' cooks and plied her with spices to use in the family meals. In return, Dutch saved JB a dessert for when he stopped by the fort kitchen most evenings. Evidently, JB had a sweet tooth.

Jack was pretty sure it was the only tooth left in his head.

When Jack heard JB's clanking belt he knew next would come Aloin, trotting around a corner and then JB, buckskin jacket fringes swaying as the old man teetered back and forth with his uneven bow-legged gait.

Maggie had thanked Jack for the small box of Whitman chocolates that had been left for her at the hospital a few days before. An unsigned card with her name neatly printed had arrived with it. At first she'd thought they might be from Seth. Blushing with embarrassment, he'd admitted he hadn't left the chocolates. But he promised to buy her a box next payday. So Jack had been Maggie's next guess. When he denied the gift, she smiled a knowing smile.

"JB," she almost whispered. "That dear old man."

"Probably stole them," Jack mumbled.

"Oh, posh," said Maggie.

She opened the box, offering one to her brother. When he refused, she decided on a soft dark chocolate, her eyes closing with the creamy strawberry pleasure of it.

"He plays his concertina on the point evenings. People throw money in his hat." She licked her fingers and replaced the lid. "He really plays quite well, you know."

Jack thought he'd jump in Lake Huron if he had to hear how well the old coot played his squeeze box one more time. Jack figured he could learn to play the dang stupid looking thing in the time it took a summer breeze to ruffle a leaf, as Grandpa Murphy used to say.

The next evening after band practice and sounding Tattoo, Jack found himself in the village. Mac needed him to pick up coffee as they had been shorted in that day's delivery. Laughing, Mac had said he was afraid of a mutiny if the men didn't have enough coffee come morning.

After picking up the burlap bag of coffee at J. W. Davis & Son and tossing it over his shoulder, Jack walked through the crowds.

With all the people coming to celebrate the Fourth of July, the island had become as gorged as Private Johnsen after winning the pie eating contest.

Carriages loaded with people clattered by. Some carriages had to pull over for minutes to let others pass in the congested traffic. Mostly couples strolled arm in arm this balmy July evening. The gentlemen wore skimmer hats and tailored jackets. The ladies' huge flowery hats seemed top-heavy to Jack. He wondered how a lady could walk upright with such a thing on her head. Soldiers sauntered with their lady friends, the ladies' small gloved hands lightly resting on the dark blue of the soldiers' arms.

Rose and lake fragrance blended like layers of a delicious, delicate summer cake. A pumpkin-hued horizon bordered Lake Huron. Cardinals and blue jays competed with the “ze ze zu ze” call of the black-throated green warbler, creating a pleasing symphony of bird song.

And through it all, Jack heard JB.

Following the wheezing melody of the concertina, Jack found himself standing at the point at the end of Water Street. As a large gathering of couples parted, there stood JB. But he didn't really stand. Because he never stopped moving. Holding the accordion-like instrument between his hands, squeezing, he swayed to and fro. He sang French songs in a rich deep voice that Jack would never have expected from someone so ugly. ‘Love songs’ Maggie would have called them. He had combed his hair. Next to Aloin on the ground sat JB's crumpled leather hat. It looked half full of gold and silver coins.

Standing close to a building, Jack listened and watched. He watched how the old man lost himself in his playing, his eyes closed, his smile reflecting his passion. How he swayed, his songs floating through the night. How it was hard to tell the difference between the man and the music.

Jack knew the feeling.

As if man and music were one and the same.

From the shadows of nightfall, Jack reminded himself he had no connection whatsoever to the old ugly coot who created music against the magic of a Mackinac Island sunset.

Muster was convened the next morning.

Seven soldiers were absent at the muster roll call. Two were sick in quarters. Two men were awaiting garrison court martials, including Seth. It was discovered two men had not returned from the village the night before so a squad was sent to bring them back.

And one man had been charged with desertion. Jack had cringed at that allegation.

He was sure he had heard about how the Never Sweats were going to beat Cheboygan the next day at least ten times before breakfast.

At daybreak on the Fourth of July, fort cannons fired the national salute of thirty-eight rounds, one round for each state of the Union. As if the island wasn't already teeming with tourists, hundreds more people arrived at the docks that morning.

A soft morning haze lingering at First Call warned of the expected afternoon heat. With most of the officers and enlisted men off to Cheboygan to cheer the Never Sweats, Dutch needed help in the kitchen. Maggie was off from the hospital, so Jack recruited her to help. She cut up watermelons, helped bake ginger snaps, and cleaned mountains of strawberries for Dutch's strawberry short cake. It had become the traditional Fourth of July dessert at the fort.

Seth had to stay in the fort jail pending his court martial on Monday. He had seemed so worried that Mac had told him he would likely get the lightest sentence possible. That had made Jack feel a little better too. That and the fact that Mac promised Seth would receive an extra big piece of strawberry shortcake that night.

When Jack told Maggie he was too old to take part in all the games in the village, she had told him 'posh'. She said she was older than him and she still enjoyed it all.

Never had Jack seen a Fourth of July celebration like on Mackinac Island. It was like an Ohio harvest celebration and Christmas all rolled into one. Maggie and Inga took part in the jumping contest. Jack hadn't been pleased to see Inga at first. But he decided he wouldn't let it bother him today.

Everything would have been better if Seth could have been here.

Maggie dared Jack to enter the greased pole climbing contest. Jack surprised himself when he turned to Inga and said he would enter the contest if she would, making her laugh.

He hadn't really heard her laugh before, Jack realized. He liked it. It didn't sound stupid like he thought it would. It sort of sounded like flowers looked. And somehow her nose didn't look as small. And her eyes crinkled in a sort of pretty way when she laughed.

Surprising himself again, Jack decided to 'have at it' in the tightrope walking contest between the town docks. After three wobbly steps, he plummeted the short distance into the shallow harbor waters joining several others. Ten-year-old Billy Grimms of the village was the only one to make it across.

Jack decided he would win the rowing contest instead.

"I thought you didn't like small boats" Maggie yelled through the crowd noise.

"That's what YOU think," Jack yelled back.

And you're right, he thought, forcing a smile. But he was still determined to overcome this fear. Besides, he told himself more than once, the contest didn't take place far from shore.

And several of his buddies from the Round Island trip watched from the docks.

He waved at Inga standing with Maggie on the docks, his other hand gripping an oar as if it were his last link to life. Sweat stung his eyes. He ignored the shiver down his back.

Sun lit Jack's hair into a fiery red mass. The uneven splashes of oars dipping into the water from the assortment of contestants were overshadowed by screams of delight from another contest.

Just as the contest was about to start, Jack spotted him.

Daniel sat three boats over at the start line, dapper as always in his staw hat. Jack watched as Daniel's toothy grin targeted a petite brunette twirling a pink parasol on the docks.

With the ready, set and pistol firing, the rowers were off.

Calling upon every muscle in his body, Jack heaved the oars with a vigor and strength above the rest. It didn't matter if he won the contest.

As long as he beat Daniel.

Jack pulled up next to Daniel. Sneering, Daniel freed one hand from an oar, tipped his hat and grabbed the edge of Jack's boat, rocking it wildly.

Spectators laughed and clapped at what they perceived was a clownish joke between two friends.

Smiling through his watery dread, oars gripped tight in both hands, Jack summoned all his strength to free his boat and jerked ahead of Daniel.

His plan had worked.

Jack crossed the finish line third, four boats ahead of Daniel.

Jack spent from mid-afternoon on playing in the fort military band. That meant he missed Dutch's special holiday dinner at the fort altogether. But he didn't miss the hubbub of the Never Sweats returning victorious from Cheboygan. They had won their game seventeen to ten, and were twenty-five dollars the richer for it.

What looked to Jack like thousands of people, well-dressed tourists as well as everyday folk, filled the piers for the fireworks over the lake that night. Andrew Chesapeake burned his hand lighting a firework. Doc Bailey saw to it. By the time Jack returned to the fort, it had been dark for some time.

Sitting in a chair next to the kitchen stove, Jack was pretty sure he would never get up again. He'd sore feet from walking barefoot on the rocky beach and his face shone a golden brown. His arms already ached from the rowing contest. He smiled with that memory.

Jack figured he wouldn't likely be able to lift a fife tomorrow.

Spending time with Inga hadn't been that horrible. Maggie had mentioned something about an outing with the four of them as soon as Seth became available.

Remembering Inga's laughter, the pink flowers of her dress, Jack hadn't said no.

This had been a day to remember.

Jack decided he deserved some of Dutch's strawberry shortcake. Cutting himself a piece big enough to compensate for missing dinner, he sank his teeth into the first bite with an enormous sigh. Fool was let out for the last time before bed.

Moonlight glinted gold off of Fool as he ran along what had become his path behind the barracks. An errant reveler from the village voiced his excitement; cricket chirps ruled the night while rose and wildflower scents soothed.

But Jack's mind was not on the beauty surrounding him.

When the deserter had been announced at Muster that morning, Jack's heart had twisted in pain.

They must have announced his father as a deserter at a Muster many years ago. To hear it said out loud made it real. He really did have a father once who swung Maggie to the sky and made her laugh. Who laughed with her. Who may have laughed with him as a babe.

Jack wished he could remember his father. But he couldn't.

The only thing he could do now to connect with his father was to make his name honorable again.

— 15 —

"Only you, little man"

JB followed Jack like bad luck follows a broken mirror.

At least it felt that way to Jack.

If JB saw Jack and Fool sitting on the barracks porch, Jack practicing his fife or bugle, JB would amble over in his crooked, bow-legged manner, Aloin at his heels, and sit near him. It looked and smelled like the old coot had finally bathed, but Jack still didn't want to take any chances sitting next to him.

Some kind of little critter might jump on him. Bite him.

Sometimes JB would just fill and smoke the long thin pipe he carried and not say a word.

Jack didn't like the old man sitting near him, but he usually ignored him. Or willed him to leave. Jack had learned if he got up to leave, the old man would eventually show up wherever he was. Nobody seemed to mind the old man in the kitchen or even in the barracks. But JB didn't like being indoors. Jack discovered he even slept outdoors behind Island House. It was just his way.

"You loyal, little man," JB had said out of the blue one day not long after the Fourth of July weekend. He'd nodded with himself in agreement. "You come for get me, yes?"

Jack figured out what he was talking about.

"My friend had to spend a week in jail and pay a five dollar fine because I went to get you." Jack enunciated the last few words and stopped himself from saying 'old man' out loud.

JB shrugged and drew on his pipe. "You loyal."

Jack figured he'd be an old man himself if he waited for a 'thank you' from the old coot.

And he surely wouldn't be doing anything 'loyal' again for the old man any time soon.

Sitting alone in the middle of Ste. Anne's Church, Jack missed his grandmother's rosary.

Maggie had cried last Sunday when he'd gently pressed the cool smooth beads into her hands during Mass. She'd admired them when Jack first showed them to her in May. He should have given them to her then. But he couldn't. Somehow now it felt right.

He'd decided to give them to her in church so she wouldn't make a scene. He'd even added that plea to his last prayer. She didn't really blubber cry, but she had to keep wiping her tears and she sniffled a lot. His shoulder had become soggy on the walk home as she kept leaning her head on it, smoothing the beads between her fingers. Thanking him.

It had been the right thing to do, Jack knew.

Maggie had probably never told a lie in her life. She'd been a good daughter to their mother. She'd been left behind by their grandparents, yet she still lit candles for them. She cared about JB. She took care of sick and hurt soldiers in the hospital.

And she didn't begrudge their father for his disappearance.

Jack knew he'd never deserved the rosary with its fine St. Patrick's Celtic crucifix. The smooth pale green marble beads. Maybe he shouldn't have taken them in the first place.

Maybe he was just supposed to bring them here to Maggie all along.

But he missed them beneath his pillow at night. Missed their scent, the cool constant reverence of them.

It would probably be easier to leave the island without them anyway, he'd told himself. One less reminder of another time and place. Another life.

Here he sat in Ste. Anne's church on a Saturday afternoon. Father St. Denis had just heard his confession. Jack's fingers bumbled with their efforts to pray without the rosary. He'd established a certain rhythm with it; a click and stroke, click and stroke, when saying his Hail Marys and Our Fathers.

Kneeling in the hard wooden pew, he focused on his

prayer. But his mind wandered to last night's dream. He couldn't shake free of it. It haunted him, even in church.

Grandpa Murphy. Jack hadn't dreamed of him since leaving Ohio. But there he'd stood in Jack's' dream: tall, ruddy complexioned, white haired and robust. The way Jack remembered him best.

Jack had wanted to ask his grandpa so many questions in the dream—about his father and mother—about Grandma—but his words wouldn't come. Did he know Jack had taken care of Pete? About the garden he grew now? His grandpa had spoken to him in the dream, but when Jack awoke in a breathless sweat, his heart pounding in his throat, the words had evaporated.

Upon awaking from his dream, Jack had reached for his fiddle under his bed. He wasn't sure why. Just as he wasn't sure why the word 'forgive' crackled in his brain all day long until Jack had found himself at confession. He hadn't planned to come. Not until tomorrow with Maggie. He'd just found himself walking toward Ste. Anne's.

Forgive what, Jack wondered. Was his grandfather asking Jack to forgive him for dying? For not telling Jack the truth about his father? For leaving Maggie behind so many years ago?

Jack's empty fingers moved back and forth in a practiced manner. Just as he figured he should be leaving, he heard it from the back pews.

A hoarse, high-pitched voice telling Aloin to stay outside.

Jack started interjecting a prayer that JB wouldn't see him between his Hail Marys and Our Fathers.

Jack couldn't help but overhear in the hush of the church. Father St. Denis was greeting JB now, welcoming him. Telling him how good it was to see him again even though JB had been there only two evenings past. As Jack heard the good father thank the old coot for the monies, he heard jingling and Father St. Denis commending JB for his devotion to the church. Praising and petting Aloin on the porch.

JB mumbled something and then the two spoke French for a minute before Father St. Denis walked slowly up the aisle past Jack toward the sanctuary, the swish of his cassock loud within the quiet reverence of church.

Jack waited. If he walked out, he would have to pass JB in one of the back pews. Jack wondered if the old man had followed him here since he seemed to show up about everywhere else he went. Probably sat in the back in fear if he sat too close to the front he might be struck by lightening, Jack figured.

Probably not, Jack thought. Father had spoken kindly to JB. Thanked him for his piety.

Jack bristled. Was he receiving a harsher penance than the old . . . ? If Father listened to JB's confession, he would no doubt know why the old man gave so much money to the church. The man was a thief. And had likely done worse in his day.

Ste. Anne's touched Jack like no other place he'd been. At home the school had doubled as church on Sundays and the traveling priest only visited Kendall Plains once a month at most.

Lemon oil and wood smells comforted Jack. The serene hush of prayer from the sparsely scattered worshippers reminded him of the lake murmuring to shore, a sound that had been unknown to him only a few short months ago. The sanctuary twinkled with a sea of tiny lights from the fragile beauty of votive candles burning for glory and remembrance. Dust motes played within the dusky sunrays streaming through the colorful stained glass windows. Like angels cascading to earth, Jack thought.

He wrenched his fingernail from his teeth and hunched lower in the pew when he heard JB's clanging. As the old man ambled past his pew on his way to light a candle, Jack sneaked down the aisle and out the open double church door, barely slowing to give Aloin a pat on the head.

"All's well," the sentry called.

Jack heard a clanking and he knew. All was *not* well.

Sure enough, Aloin came trotting in the open kitchen door, his tail now wagging at the sight of Fool. A soldier wasn't allowed into the fort this late without knowing the password, but somehow JB just came and went as he pleased.

Nothing about that old man seemed fair.

As soon as JB stepped through the doorway, Jack knew he was drunk. The old man wove his way to a stool at a work table, his rear end connecting with it on the third try.

Jack rose to leave. He didn't want to be around him when he was sober. He sure didn't want to be around him now. Then he realized if he left, the old man might pass out. Jack didn't want Dutch finding JB's stinky old body on the kitchen floor come morning. Dutch didn't deserve that.

Nobody deserved that.

Lifting his straggly head from the table, JB's bloodshot eyes bore into Jack.

"Ahh, petit homme," JB slurred. " J'ai faim. Je suis votre grand-père."

Dang it, thought Jack.

"I don't know what you said, old man, but you have to leave."

It didn't bother Jack one bit to call him old man now.

JB sniffed and offered his hand. "Some food?"

"You have money to buy food," snapped Jack. "You don't have to come beggin' here."

JB's head landed back on the table. Jack figured the only way to get rid of him was to feed him. He gave him a slab of meat and a piece of bread from Dutch's larder. He figured the old man couldn't be thirsty with all he'd had to drink.

JB gave his meat to Aloin and nibbled at the bread. Sighing, Jack got another slab of meat for JB and a bowl of water for Aloin.

Wasn't the dog's fault JB was his master.

"Merci, little man," JB said through bread mush. "And Aloin too thank you, eh, Aloin?"

Aloin barked and Jack immediately shushed him with

another slice of meat.

JB's eyes rested on Jack with small sharpness. "You come. We go Nort, we trap and money we make, little man," JB crooned. "You got strong back. . . we. . ." JB hurriedly felt around his belt. He removed a small round leather case, opening it for Jack. "This mon boussole." He pushed it toward Jack. "I give it. Always it help you find home."

Jack saw it was an old compass. The kerosene lantern glow cast a demon-like shadow across JB's craggy features. What did this old man know about home?

"I'm not going anywhere, ever with you, old coot. No matter what you give me."

"Oooohhweee," JB slapped at his knee and missed. "You not kind like you papa, eh, little man?"

Jack stopped. "What about my father?"

JB stuffed bread in his face as his beady eyes met Jack's.

"You papa, he with me go and we trap and we gonna beaucoup money make and. . . " An enormous sigh deflated him. His shoulders shrank, slumped into his body. His head fell onto the table. When he sat up, tears streamed through his brush of whiskers, down his neck. "You papa need money for Amelie. . . mon babe, Amelie." JB sobbed, his head resting in his hands. "I never her see again."

Reaching across the table, Jack grabbed JB's arm, pulling at him. "What about my father?"

The eyes that met Jack's had been to hell and back. "I kill him dead."

Jack froze.

JB fought for words. "I tell him, I tell him, Irish man, we not gone long. You come back and. . . " JB's voice dropped. "But he not come back." JB's sobs rattled the table. "Je regrette. Je regrette."

Jack's open mouth remained soundless. Like in the nightmare one never forgets.

"You papa, he. . . " JB reached for Jack; Jack avoided his hand. "He sit by fire. . . " JB became animated with explanation, ". . . and mon rifle she needs cleaning and I . . . he moved and . . ." He stopped, looking straight at Jack. "I shoot Irish man. On accident." He sobbed, his arms positioned as if cradling someone. "In mon arms, he is gone."

Jagged waves of cold burst through Jack. Sweat soaked his brow. He thought to breathe.

"You killed my father?"

JB heaved sobs. "Je regrette."

"My father isn't a deserter." Jack spoke with quiet authority. His eyes glistened with a sudden truth. "Why didn't you tell them. When you came back? Why didn't you tell her?"

JB shrugged. "I not. . . not come here for many years. After." He looked older and smaller. "Je suis. . . coward."

"You just. . . you just left him?" Jack's chest heaved with his words. "You. . . let them all think he deserted? Didn't my mother know he was with you?"

JB's chin rested on his caved chest and he became

difficult to understand. "Non. . . Amelie. . . she not know. Irish man just say he go few days. . . " His voice drifted into nothing. "You only know, little man." He sighed huge. "You only."

Grabbing JB's arm from underneath, Jack attempted to lift him.

"Don't pass out, old man," Jack's voice had become hoarse. "We have to go tell Captain Brady right now. You have to tell him the truth!"

Barely lifting his head, JB spoke in a rasp. "I die in prison. If you tell."

Standing, steadying himself by the table, JB wiped his face with his sleeves. He faced Jack. "You and me. . . we blood together." Shaking his head, he staggered to the door. "You do what you do, little man."

JB stumbled through the door, Aloin trotting after.

The compass glistened on the table.

The sentry cried, "All's well."

— 16 —

"Fool! Fool!"

Jack hadn't eaten much but it didn't matter.

He hadn't slept much and it didn't matter.

He was supposed to be working fatigue duty in the garden this morning and that didn't matter.

It didn't even matter that he was rowing a boat with just him and Fool over to Round Island without having told a soul that he had the boat or where he was going with it.

Nothing mattered right now.

He just needed time alone with his dog. Away from everything and everybody.

July sunrise arrived early on Mackinac Island so Jack had left early. Blue sky canopied muggy unmoving air. He'd rowed across the lake before with Seth and others. He could do it again. And if he got in trouble for leaving and taking the boat without permission, he would face it like a man.

He wasn't a coward.

Making Fool lay down in the middle of the rowboat, Jack tried to concentrate on Round Island to stay his fears of the water.

But his thoughts kept returning to the night before in the kitchen.

All these years his grandparents had thought their son a deserter. His mother thought she had been deserted. Left with two young children to raise on her own.

Maggie. She loved JB. But she would want the truth to be told. To have their father's good name restored.

Jack's tangled thoughts stayed with him until he found he'd reached shore. Recalling his nightmare of long ago, he felt he'd conquered his fear of drowning.

But he had other fears to reckon with.

His eyes filled as he thought of his Grandpa Murphy, as big and strong as JB was small and weak. Jack truly believed his father's death was an accident. But he didn't think he could ever forgive JB for letting people think Sean Michael Murphy had deserted his family and duty.

Jack dragged his rowboat onto the beach. He would be back by supper and pay whatever price had to be paid for leaving.

He recalled what JB had said about the price he would pay. Prison. If Jack turned JB in, would he even admit to it? There were no witnesses. The old man was drunk and had confessed that Jack was the only other person he'd ever told.

Sunlight filtered through the dense treetops in the middle of the island. The cool shade refreshed him some.

Jack sat on an old tree that had long ago fallen onto the forest floor, Fool laying close by. Part of Jack just wanted to go somewhere with Fool and never have to come back to face this.

Boston. He could take off to Boston and he wouldn't have to tell a soul there about JB. He was planning on going there anyway. Maybe he should just leave now. Mac or Seth would loan him train fare.

He snapped a small branch in two. Kept snapping its twigs off in a comforting rhythm.

Maggie. He came to find Maggie and to regain honor for his father's name. His name. The first had been accomplished, and by tonight the other could be as well. Maggie had claimed she didn't care. That she would always love Papa anyway.

But she should know.

A bolt of regret zapped through him with the thought of leaving his sister and friends.

Fool chased squirrels. Jack thought through the different possibilities of telling Captain Brady about JB. And about not telling him. Or anyone. Would his father have wanted the old man to die in prison?

His father must have liked the old man to go off with him like that. If JB had come back and told them about the accident, it might have been all right. He might have been forgiven. But he didn't. His hiding the truth had turned the truth into shame.

A man's honor was at stake. No, Jack realized. The honor of two men was at stake.

And no matter how he tried to figure it, one man's honor would become the other man's shame.

His head hurt. He was tired and hungry. Finding a soft niche in the cool forest floor, Jack welcomed the escape of sleep.

Jack awoke to darkness.

He knew he couldn't have slept more than an hour or two. As he and Fool left the woods for the beach, he saw that thick bubbling black clouds had replaced the white fluffy ones, just as a stiff cool wind had replaced the warm breeze.

Across the lake, Mackinac Island lights flickered like cheery little candles. Jack knew he had to leave now. Never had he seen a storm come in this fast. But it wasn't raining yet and he was sure he could make it across the darkening harbor before it did.

He'd done it before.

Commanding Fool to lie down in the boat, Jack boosted them off from shore.

Water that had seemed a bit choppy near shore became rougher the further out he rowed. Wind whipped his hat off. Water spray stung his face. When he yelled at a prancing Fool to lie down, he could barely hear his own voice through the waves and wind. Gloom chased them like a hungry glowering giant.

Lightening crackled, illuminating the island, making it seem closer. Thunder shook his boat before rain pellets battered him without mercy, water creeping up Jack's boots.

The Island House lights in his direct line of sight glowed like a beacon to guide him.

"Stay down, Fool!" he yelled through the crashes and rattles that sounded like a freight train rumbling by.

Trying to bail water with one hand, Jack thrashed about trying to soothe a whining Fool. Jack fought the oars for control as whitecaps rolled at him, lifted him, dipped him into wells.

Closer, he knew he was getting closer. Once he reached the harbor, the water would settle down. Almost there. Black skies lowered, a bolt of lightening just missing their bow. Fool rocked the boat in his desperation to escape.

Jack heard voices calling from Mackinac Island. Wiping rain from his eyes, he searched its shore hard.

When he turned back, Fool was gone.

"Fool! Fool!"

Jack jumped into the lake, water rushing up his nose, into his mouth. He clung to the boat's edge.

"Fool!" Jack's tears and screams were soundless in the storm.

There! Fool! Bobbing a few feet away. Paddling towards him. Barking. A wave doused Jack's rising joy.

Voices from shore. Closer.

Fool was scared. Fool needed him. Jack called him but the dog seemed to be drifting farther away.

Jack let go.

Submerged, water filled Jack's lungs. When he surfaced, coughing, choking, he listened for Fool. Thunder and wind battered the dark. Waves sucked at him, slapped at him. Screams echoed from shore.

His voice rasped raw through his tears. "Fool!"
The beckoning lights of the Island House vanished.

— 17 —

"You look good to all da ladies dear"

"Fool!"

"Doctor!"

Fuzzy light hurt Jack's eyes. He closed them. It felt like the Fourth of July was exploding inside his head. Maggie?

"Jack?"

Opening his eyes, he turned from the light. Someone was pulling down the window blinds. He felt a weight next to him as someone sat. He was lying on a bed.

"It's good to see you awake, young man," said Doctor Bailey. "We were a bit concerned about you."

Jack forced himself to look around the room. He was in a hospital bed. The post hospital. He'd been somewhere . . . in a boat . . . a storm . . .

"Fool!" When he tried to sit up, a blinding pain thrust him backwards.

"Now, just stay put, Jack." The doctor's voice sounded far away. "Your dog made it to shore. He's with Dutch resting up."

The weight beside him lifted.

Soft hands adjusted the thick white bandage wrapped around his head. Maggie was so close he could see her warm hazel eyes clearly, her tight smile as a single tear dribbled off her chin onto his face.

"Oh, I'm sorry, Jack," she sniffed and laughed. "I'm getting you all wet. I. . . " She turned and Jack could see her shoulders shake from behind.

Fool made it to shore, he thought.

Doc Bailey stood next to the bed. "Tell me what you remember, Son."

Closing his eyes, Jack tried to concentrate. He had gone to Round Island for something. . . to think about something. . . with Fool and. . . Jack's eyes flew open. JB! He had gone to think about what JB had told him. About his father.

"All I remember is. . . rowing back in a storm and Fool got scared and, I heard voices from shore and. . . I was looking at the Island House lights to help guide me and . . . Fool was gone and . . . " He looked from Maggie to Doc Bailey then closed his eyes. Talking made his head hurt more. "How did I get here?"

"Your grandfather brought you to shore, Jack," said the doctor.

Jack bristled at hearing JB called his grandfather.

"He . . . JB had come to the fort that day looking for Captain Brady who was in St. Ignace," the doctor continued. "Mac told JB it was suspected you had taken one of the fort boats and gone off somewhere since Fool was gone too."

Jack looked at the doctor waiting for more.

"Word is. . . " the doctor cleared his throat, "word is JB was working at the Island House that afternoon, putting porch chairs away because of the storm, when he saw a capsized boat in the harbor. He. . . " here the doctor sighed and raised his chin to finish, "he swam out and pulled you to shore. Carried you back."

Jack snorted and his head hurt. "I expect the old coot will be wanting my thanks."

Moving his feet, Jack felt something at the bottom of his bed. Heard a wheezing noise. Raising his head slightly, he saw it came from inside a small round box.

"Jack," the doctor said softly.

Jack looked for Maggie. She'd turned from him.

"His heart gave out, Son," the doctor said. "It was all just. . . too much for him." Jack waited, wanting more. But there was no more.

JB had died saving his life.

"We were. . . we thought he'd have wanted you to have this," the doctor said, bringing the boxed concertina to the head of Jack's bed. "You being musically inclined like him."

His hand on top of the box, Jack stared at the ceiling.

"It was. . . a lovely service. . . a mass. . . at Ste. Anne's," Doctor Bailey said. "Mrs. Van Allen of the Island House took care of the coffin and. . . there was an abundance of flowers. It seems many of the people he worked with and . . . others gave toward the service."

Jack stared up at Doctor Bailey.

"And," continued the doctor, "Sergeant MacDougal

played the bagpipes since you were unable. . . we thought you might have played if. . . it was a lovely service. Well attended."

"He's buried?" Jack whispered in disbelief. It seemed like he had just been rowing in a storm. The waves. Sitting at the kitchen table with JB. "What. . . how long ago did . . . was the storm?"

"You've been here almost a week, Son," the doctor explained. "You must have hit your head on the boat. A concussion like yours takes time to heal." Doctor Bailey paused. "He's buried in Ste. Anne's cemetery next to your mother. Maggie thought that best."

Moon and stars glittered in the black lake. Nothing in Jack's view from the fort's West Blockhouse suggested there was life below in the stillness and heat of the one o'clock hour. But he knew it was there. There was life below. There was death below.

And here he stood.

Jack figured someone had seen him come here from the barracks. But he'd been here for some time now and nobody had told him to leave. He'd been back in the barracks for a few days and everyone had been so kind to him. He hadn't had to work much. Everyone wanted to make sure he was feeling all right. The doctor checked on him daily. Mac came by. Seth asked how he was doing a couple times a day. And Maggie.

All on account of JB dying.

Jack smiled small.

The old coot was as much a pain in the neck dead as he had been alive. Yet Jack had to wonder. Why had JB come to the fort looking for Captain Brady the day of the storm? Unless his intent had been to confess to accidentally killing Sean Murphy all those years ago.

Jack would never know for sure. All he could do was wonder.

Sighing, he focused on a star; watched its sparkle ebb, then brighten. A beacon to guide lost souls in the dark.

He'd thought about leaving. Going to Boston. If he left, he wouldn't have to deal with any of this. He could just leave it all behind.

But he wasn't a coward. Or was he? He hadn't told anyone about JB and his father. Not yet. He'd started to tell Maggie once, but couldn't. He wasn't sure why. JB was dead, so couldn't he tell Captain Brady and have his father's good name restored? Isn't that why he had come to this island?

Maggie had told Jack JB's real name: Jean Baptiste Roy. Jack had always thought he had been named after his father. Sean meant John or Jack in Ireland.

Jack watched another star glimmer then disappear.

He'd found out Jean meant the same in French.

Jack chuckled. "Maggie said you were all cleaned up in your coffin, with new clothes and such. Wish I could have seen that." Smiling, he mimicked JB's speech. "You look good to all da ladies dear, eh?"

A husky rasp penetrated Jack's voice.

"Aloin. . . he wouldn't eat. He..." trembling, Jack fought tears, "...he stayed with you until they put you in the ground, old man. They said he slept by your coffin and. . . then he wouldn't leave your grave until they made him."

Pounding the wall with a fist, he laughed high pitched and hard into the night. "There's your loyalty!"

'All's well' echoed through the night.

"Blast it to hell!" Jack swore. "You think you've made it all better, don't you, old man? You think because you saved my life. . . it's all better. Well. . . " he fought for words, needing to say them out loud so JB could hear them. "Saving my life," Jack thumped his chest, "doesn't make up for killing my father! It doesn't!"

He followed a night hawk's journey from treetop to treetop in the moonlight. Watched it glide gracefully in dark and silence.

"Why did you have to tell me?" he begged of the night. "Why. . . didn't you tell someone else? Did you think I wouldn't tell because we are. . . 'blood loyal', stupid old . . ." wavering, Jack stopped. Wetting his lips, he stuttered a laugh. "You know, I should be closer to the ground where you probably are, right old man? Here I am, talking to the heavens and. . . likely you're on the other end of things."

Sighing, Jack hung his head. No, he thought. No. JB had saved his life. Jack backed to the inside corner of the blockhouse as his thoughts swirled. JB had taken the life of

Sean Murphy but saved the life of his son.

Was regaining one man's honor worth compromising that of another?

Opening his left hand, Jack offered his compass to the moon.

18

"Forgive?"

A small bouquet of violets, buttercups and wood lilies graced each of the graves. Jack's mother's headstone appeared weathered next to JB's new one.

Jack had finally received his first soldier's pay.

Fool and Aloin stayed close to Jack. He wondered if they knew where they were.

Or why.

He'd thought about inviting Maggie after all the times she'd offered to bring him here to see their mother's grave. But he'd changed his mind. He needed to be alone.

It seemed strange but comforting speaking to his mother like this.

But for some reason, talking to JB seemed normal. It made him feel like everyday life at the fort when JB used to follow him around, sit next to him and smoke his pipe, spend time in the kitchen with Dutch.

Jack had thought about everything that had happened

until his brain was mush. He'd never know if JB had planned on confessing about Sean Murphy's death when he went to the fort looking for Captain Brady the day of the storm.

But Jack had to think so.

His dream kept to the fore of his thoughts. He'd not been able to hear Grandpa Murphy's voice before. But now Jack heard the Irish brogue rich and strong in his mind.

Forgive.

And Jack knew.

"I'm learning to play your squeeze box, old man." Jack laughed. "It's harder than it looks."

Sighing, Jack smiled. His unfolding fingers revealed JB's compass.

"I won't be needing this anymore."

He thought of this place, this island. His friends. Family. How blue of sky magically became one with blue of lake. The welcoming peace of it. Like a tune well played.

"I've found my way home."

Placing the compass on JB's grave, he spoke the promise aloud.

"I won't tell."

Jack smiled.

"Grandpa."

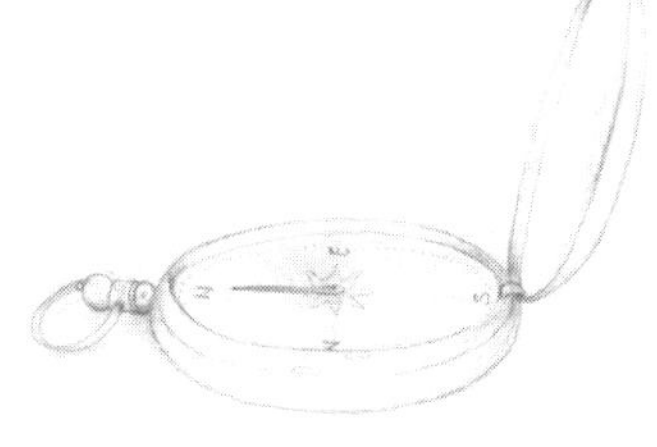

Epilogue

Fort Mackinac
Mackinac Island,
Michigan
August 6th, 1885

Dear Uncle Patrick and Aunt Sarah,

I hope this letter greets you in good health. I hope you understand when I tell you I will not be coming to Boston, except maybe to visit. I was born on this island and it seems it has become my home again. I am settled at Fort Mackinac and see a comfortable future here. Please come to Mackinac Island for the wedding of my sister Maggie to Corporal Seth Anders on September 12th of this year.

But be careful! Once here, you may not ever want to leave this magical island.

Your nephew,
Jack

P.S. I have two dogs now!

The Place Behind the Story

Home to Mackinac is a fictional novel. Jack, Maggie, JB and Seth never existed. There was no young boy who enlisted at Fort Mackinac in this period. In reality, it would have been much more difficult for a fourteen-year-old to get away with what Jack did. Certain other characters, such as Dr. Bailey and Mrs. Van Allen at the Island House, did exist.

Mackinac Island is also a real place. All the places described in the book existed in the 1880s, and most of them still exist. The pattern of life at Mackinac in a Victorian summer was as it is described in the story. The daily routine at the fort, large numbers of tourists and Fourth of July events were much as found in *Home to Mackinac*.

Mackinac History

Mackinac (pronounced Mack-i-naw) Island was and is a very special place to the American Indian peoples of the Great Lakes region. Its full name is *Michilimackinac*, meaning Great Turtle. To American Indians traveling by canoe, the Island resembled a turtle, an animal sacred to them. Mackinac Island had a special place in American Indian mythology. It was the place where the world began. Only small bands of Indians lived in the Straits of Mackinac year around, but thousands came in the summer to fish.

The area was eventually part of New France. Frenchman began coming here in the middle 1600s. In 1671, the Jesuits (a Roman Catholic religious order) established a mission on the north side of the Straits of Mackinac. They named it St. Ignace. French fur traders soon began to come to the location in great numbers during the summer. A fort was eventually built at the location. The mission and fort were moved to the south side of the Straits of Mackinac in the early 1700s. Here it became known as Fort Michilimackinac. It was a main center of the fur trade throughout the 1700s.

In the 1760s, along with the rest of New France, Fort Michilimackinac came under British control. In 1780, fearing an attack by American rebels, the fort was moved from the mainland to more secure Mackinac Island. After the American Revolution it became part of the new United States. Although the British captured and held it during the War of 1812, Mackinac has remained an American place ever since. In 1837 it officially became part of the new State of Michigan.

The Fort

Fort Mackinac is on a bluff overlooking the village and harbor. The first buildings at the fort were ones moved from mainland Fort Michilimackinac in the early 1780s. None of these buildings survive. The oldest building in the fort is the Officers' Stone Quarters, begun in 1780 by the British. Fort Mackinac's three blockhouses were built in the late 1790s after the Americans took control. The remaining buildings in the fort were built throughout the 1800s. In the early years it was a strategic border fort, helping to guard the lucrative fur trade. The capture of Fort Mackinac by the British in 1812 was the first land engagement of that war in the United States, showing the fort's strategic importance. The fur trade declined in the 1830s, and Fort Mackinac became a quiet place. During the Civil War it was completely abandoned, as all the soldiers left to fight on the front lines. Life became more exciting at Fort Mackinac again after 1875 when Mackinac Island became a national park–the second national park in the country. More soldiers were dispatched to help take care of the park, as the country did not have a Park Service in those days. The soldiers were like park rangers. Fort Mackinac remained an active post until 1895. When the fort was closed, Mackinac National Park was transferred to the state. It became Mackinac Island State Park, Michigan's first state park.

The Town and People

Mackinac Island in the 1880s was reaching its peak as a premier Victorian resort. Thousands of tourists flocked to the island aboard steamships each summer. They were attracted to the coolness of its water setting, natural beauty and historic charm. It was already an old-fashioned place in the 1880s! Hotels, restaurants and souvenir shops sprang up to meet the visitors' needs. The 1880s also saw the first major construction of summer cottages on the island. Many of these were built on the island's east and west bluffs on national park property. The village is nestled along the shore below the fort. Water Street (now Main Street) and Market Street are the two main streets.

Although thousands of people came to Mackinac Island in the summer, its year around population was very small. This remains true today. Many of Mackinac Island's families are descendents of Métis people like Jack and Maggie. A wave of Irish immigrants also came to the island in the 1800s.

Mackinac Today

You can see and visit most of the places described in *Home to Mackinac*. Fort Mackinac has been restored to its appearance in the 1880s. The buildings are furnished with exhibits and there are live programs each day including cannon and rifle firings. You can go inside the Soldiers' Barracks where Jack and the soldiers lived, visit the Guard House where Seth spent his time prior to his court martial or walk the walls on your own sentry beat.

In town can still be found the Astor buildings where Maggie worked and the dance was held. Originally the buildings of the Astor House had been the fur warehouse and agent's home of the American Fur Company, built in the early 1800s. They were converted into the Astor House in the middle 1800s. In the middle 1900s they were restored to their original appearance. They are now used as the City of Mackinac Island museum and offices. Island House still operates as a hotel on Mackinac and you can also still stop in at Ste. Anne's Church, just down the street. Out in the park you can have your own picnic lunch at Devil's Kitchen or Arch Rock. If you can find a boat, you can also venture across the water to Round Island for a swim!

Read More About It

If you want to learn more about Mackinac Island and its history, we recommend the following books published by Mackinac State Historic Parks:

Dirk Gringhuis, *Lore of the Great Turtle: Indian Legends of Mackinac Retold*, 1970

Dwight H. Kelton, *Annals of Fort Mackinac*, 1992 (reprint of 1882 edition)

Phil Porter, *Mackinac: An Island Famous In These Regions*, 1998

Phil Porter, ed. *A Boy at Fort Mackinac: The Diary of Harold Dunbar Corbusier, 1883-1884, 1892*, 1994

You can find out more about Mackinac Island and Fort Mackinac on the web at MackinacParks.com.

Fort Mackinac bugler.

ABOVE: *Fort Mackinac musicians down in the village, 1880s.*

BELOW: *Soldiers on the Fort Mackinac parade ground. Buildings are, front left to right: Corner of Soldiers' Barracks, Quartermaster's Storehouse, Post Headquarters and Commissary. In the background can be seen the East Blockhouse to the left and the Post Hospital to the right.*

Front of fort from upper gun platform, 1880s.

ABOVE: *Soldiers in full dress uniform with their rifles in front of the Soldiers' Barracks. On the hill can be seen the Officers' Hill Quarters and the North Blockhouse.*

BELOW: *Inside the Squad Room on the first floor of the Soldiers' Barracks, 1880s.*

American Indians selling baskets in the village.

ABOVE: *Fort Mackinac Post Hospital.*

BELOW: *View of the Fort Mackinac garden and the west end of the village from Fort Mackinac.*

ABOVE: *The* Algomah *coming into the harbor.*

BELOW: *Round Island from Mackinac Island.*

Shops along Water Street, Fort Mackinac in the distance.

ABOVE: *The Astor House on Market Street, Fort Mackinac in the distance.*

BELOW: *The Palmer House hotel.*

Ste. Anne's Church, 1880s

ABOVE. *Summer visitors at Devil's Kitchen.*

OPPOSITE PAGE TOP: *Fort Mackinac soldiers posing on Arch Rock.*

OPPOSITE PAGE BOTTOM: *Fourth of July on Mackinac Island in the 1880s.*

MEAT MARKET
DEALERS IN EVERYTHING

ABOVE. *The Island House in about 1880.*

OPPOSITE PAGE TOP: *Fort Mackinac and the east end of the village from the west. Below the fort is the army garden. Ste. Anne's Church can be seen in the distance.*

OPPOSITE PAGE BOTTOM: *West Blockhouse in about 1900. In the distance is Grand Hotel, constructed in 1887.*

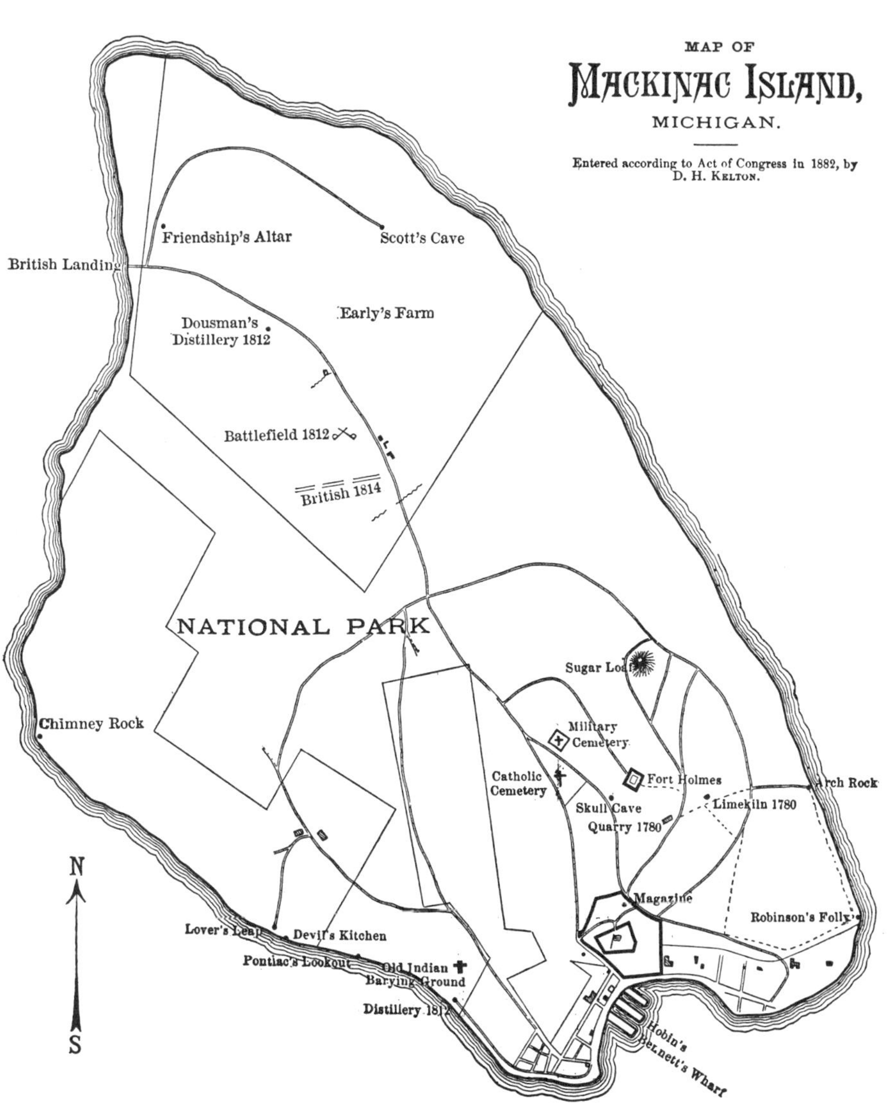
MAP OF
MACKINAC ISLAND,
MICHIGAN.
Entered according to Act of Congress in 1882, by
D. H. KELTON.
Friendship's Altar
Scott's Cave
British Landing
Early's Farm
Dousman's
Distillery 1812
Battlefield 1812
British 1814
NATIONAL PARK
Sugar Loaf
Chimney Rock
Military
Cemetery
Catholic
Cemetery
Fort Holmes
Arch Rock
Skull Cave
Limekiln 1780
Quarry 1780
N
S
Magazine
Robinson's Folly
Lover's Leap
Devil's Kitchen
Pontiac's Lookout
Old Indian
Burying Ground
Distillery 1812
Hobin's
Bennett's Wharf

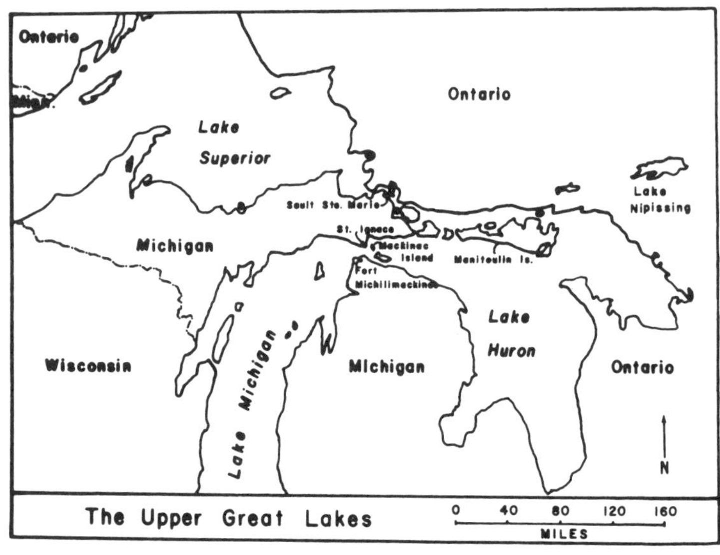

The Upper Great Lakes

Acknowledgements

The author would like to acknowledge Mackinac State Historic Parks for the privilege of writing this book, and Katherine Cederholm, for her historical research and patience with incessant questions.

Home to Mackinac is the one-hundredth title published by the Mackinac Island State Park Commission since 1962. Over the last forty-four years the Park Commission has supported this ambitious program. We are grateful to Chairman Dennis O. Cawthorne and the entire commission for fostering these publications that provide an additional venue to preserve and present the history of Mackinac.

About the Author

Born in Muskegon and raised in Detroit, Kim Delmar Cory currently lives in Lansing, Michigan, just a stone's throw from Michigan State University where she earned her Bachelor's in English Literature and Master's in Education in the 1970s. Family consists of her husband, Loren, son, Justin and daughter, Amanda, along with a menagerie of four cats and a big yellow Lab named Brutus.

Ms. Cory has taught writing classes at Lansing Community College for over fifteen years and currently advises students with disabilities there. Additionally, she teaches how to write for children through the Institute of Children's Literature. Her love for Mackinac Island takes her there several times a year and she would like to move there with her family to write and have her own horse.

About the Illustrator

Laura Evans is a free-lance artist and illustrator who loves both art and history. These two subjects naturally come together in the Mackinac Island region, which she has painted for years. Although born and raised in the Detroit area, her love of "up north" began with summers spent in northern Michigan and Canada.

The pencil drawings for this book were a delightful departure from her usual media, watercolor (front cover of the book), but allowed her to explore, imitate, and connect with illustrators she remembered from her childhood reading.

A graduate of Eastern Michigan University, she continues to live in Lower Michigan with her husband and two sons. Michael, her younger son, was the model for her first children's book, *A Castle at the Straits*, and her elder son Nicholas portrayed Jack in this book. Jammie, her Austrian Sheppard, was the model for two dogs this time!